Don't Do It!

"Please open the door!"

The girl on the other side of the door repeated her desperate plea. *"Please!"*

Lea was frozen by indecision. A frightening picture flashed into her mind. She saw a hideous monster with red eyes bulging out of its sockets and green slime drooling from its fang-filled mouth. The monster was hulking on the other side of the locked door, disguising its voice, using the voice of a frightened girl in order to fool Lea.

"Please open the door!" the muffled voice, now even more frightened and desperate, called out to Lea.

"I-I'll be right back," Lea replied.

She had made her decision. She had decided to unlock the door.

Books by R. L. Stine

Available from ARCHWAY Paperbacks

FEAR STREET
R·L·STINE

The Secret Bedroom

AN ARCHWAY PAPERBACK
Published by POCKET BOOKS

New York London Toronto Sydney Tokyo Singapore

AN ARCHWAY PAPERBACK *Original*

An Archway Paperback published by
POCKET BOOKS, a division of Simon & Schuster Inc.
1230 Avenue of the Americas, New York, NY 10020

Copyright © 1991 by Parachute Press, Inc.

ISBN: 0-671-72483-5

First Archway Paperback printing September 1991

15 14 13 12 11

FEAR STREET is a registered trademark of Parachute Press, Inc.

AN ARCHWAY PAPERBACK and colophon are registered trademarks of Simon & Schuster Inc.

Cover art by Bill Schmidt

Printed in the U.S.A.

IL 6+

The Secret Bedroom

chapter
1

*L*ea Carson tripped and her lunch tray went flying out of her hands.

As she struggled to regain her balance, she watched the tray sail toward a crowded table. Almost as if it were happening in slow motion, Lea saw it hit the side of a girl's chair. Then she watched helplessly as the bowl toppled off the tray and the dark chili poured onto the sleeve of the girl's white sweater.

The girl screamed and leapt to her feet, her hands flying up like two startled white birds trying to escape. She shook her shoulders, then began grabbing at her sleeve, pulling off red beans and chunks of tomato.

The girl turned angrily toward Lea. Everyone at the table, a couple of astonished-looking boys and a girl with a disapproving frown, turned to glare at Lea. Lea could feel her face reddening, growing hot.

Why did I have to take chili? she thought. Why couldn't I have just picked a sandwich?

"My new sweater!" the girl cried, still scraping and pulling at the sleeve. She had wavy red hair, cut stylishly short, and pale blue eyes that flashed angrily at Lea, then back to her sweater.

"I'm sorry," Lea managed to say. "There was something wet on the floor. I slipped."

"I'd better go put some cold water on it," the girl said, ignoring Lea's apology, ignoring Lea entirely. She turned and stalked past Lea, deliberately staring straight ahead.

"I'm really sorry," Lea called after her.

Holding her stained sweater sleeve, the girl hurried through the lunchroom doors without turning back.

Lea heard laughter at another table and knew they were laughing at her. She bent down to pick up her tray, feeling all eyes on her.

I just want to die, she thought.

Only my second week in this school, and I've already made a total fool of myself.

It was hard enough, she thought, for someone as shy as she was to adjust to a new high school, to make new friends, to feel comfortable. Sure, she was pretty enough. Cute, everyone said, with her sparkling green eyes and her dark brown hair cut in a shaggy pixie style with bangs that grazed her eyebrows.

Lea has a great smile, everyone always said. Her smile lights up her face.

Well, she hadn't had much to smile about at Shadyside High. The kids all seemed so snooty and stuck-up. And now she had tripped in front of half the school and poured chili all over that red-haired girl in the white sweater.

"Here," a voice said, startling Lea from her thoughts. "Have a handful of salad."

"Oh." It was one of the boys from the table. He had picked up Lea's tray and was scooping up the remains of her lunch. "Thanks," Lea said uncertainly.

He grinned at her as she took the tray from him. She could feel her face grow hot again.

He's cute, Lea thought.

Not really handsome. But cute. He had a friendly, open face with curly brown hair and brown eyes. He was short, like Lea, not very muscular, very boyish looking. He was wearing a maroon and gray Shadyside High sweatshirt over faded jeans.

He retrieved Lea's silverware from the floor and deposited it on the tray. "That looked like good chili," he said, still grinning.

They were both squatting down below the tabletop, Lea holding the tray as he continued tossing lunch remains on it. Lea licked her lips, a nervous habit she just couldn't break. "I slipped," she said.

Well, *duh*, she thought. That was pretty obvious, wasn't it?

"Marci'll get over it," he said reassuringly. But then he added, "In a hundred years or so." His grin faded.

"She was really mad," Lea said.

That's obvious too! she scolded herself. Why do you have to sound like such a dweeb?

"She's a redhead," he said, as if that explained anything.

They both stood up. He wiped his hands on his jeans and looked to the lunchroom door. Marci hadn't returned. The other kids at the table had left.

"You're new here," he said, staring into her eyes, studying her.

"Yeah. This is my second week," Lea said uncomfortably, holding on to the tray with both hands. "Next week will probably be better," she added wryly.

"What's your name?"

"Lea. Lea Carson."

"I don't know any Leas," he said, pulling the bottom of his sweatshirt down over his wiry frame. "I'm Don Jacobs. You've probably heard of me. I'm the guy who picks the salad up from the floor."

Lea laughed. He waited for her to say something, but she couldn't think of anything to say.

I hate being shy, she thought. Hate it, hate it, hate it.

He looked toward the lunchroom door again, then back to her. "You a senior?"

"No. Junior."

"Whose homeroom?"

She licked her lips. She had to think. "Mr. Robbins."

"Where do you live?"

"On Fear Street," Lea told him. "A few blocks from the old cemetery."

"Fear Street?"

Lea was already used to this startled reaction from people when they heard where she lived. "My parents just *love* to fix up old houses," she explained. "When my dad was transferred here to Shadyside, they bought the shabbiest place they could find. They'll spend years making it beautiful, and then he'll be transferred again."

Lea sighed and glanced at a table by the wall, where

4

Deena Martinson, her lunch spread out in front of her, gave Lea a little wave. She followed it up with a wide-eyed look of surprise as she noticed who Lea was with. So far, Deena was the only friend Lea had made at Shadyside.

"My friend is waving at me," she told Don awkwardly. "It's getting late. I'd better get a new lunch and join her."

"I hear the chili's real good," he said with a straight face.

"Thanks for helping me," Lea said.

She started to move toward the food line, but he reached out and held her arm. "Since you're new here and everything," he said, his eyes darting toward the doorway, "I mean, would you like to go to a movie or something Saturday night?" He scratched his curly, brown hair and gave her his most winning, boyish grin.

Lea was practically startled speechless, but she managed to utter a yes. She stood awkwardly grinning at him, trying to think of something else to say.

"Good," he said, but then his expression quickly changed. Lea followed his gaze to the doorway, where Marci stood, arms crossed over her chest, glaring at the two of them.

"Later," Don said, and hurried off to join Marci.

Lea hurried to the food line. Maybe my lonely days here are over, she thought happily, her hands unsteady as she dropped the soiled tray onto the pile and took a clean one. Thinking about Don, about how funny he looked scrounging around on the floor to help retrieve her lunch, she picked up a tuna-fish sandwich and a box of apple juice and hurried to join Deena.

"What were you and Don Jacobs talking about?" Deena asked, wiping crumbs off her chin with a paper napkin.

"Oh, mainly about how I spilled my lunch all over that girl standing there in the doorway with him," Lea told her, plopping down across the table from her.

"You spilled your lunch on Marci Hendryx, and I missed it?" Deena cried with an expression of exaggerated disappointment.

Deena had a fragile-looking, heart-shaped face framed by very fine blond hair that she wore down to her collar. She was always complaining about how pale she was and how she couldn't do anything with her hair because it was so fine, but she was actually very pretty.

Deena had probably always played an angel in the elementary school Christmas pageants, Lea thought on first meeting her.

"Don seems nice," Lea said, taking a tentative bite of her sandwich, trying to decide whether or not to tell Deena that he'd asked her out for Saturday night. Finally she decided there was *no way* she could keep from telling her!

"He's very nice," Deena said, watching over Lea's shoulder as Marci and Don talked heatedly in the lunchroom doorway. "Everyone likes Don. He's just one of those guys when you meet him, you like him. He has a million friends."

"And girlfriends?" Lea asked.

"Just Marci." Deena turned her glance on Lea.

"Don and Marci," she said, making a face. "Man, does she keep him on a tight leash."

"Huh?" Lea practically choked on her sandwich.

"They've been going together since we were in preschool, I think," Deena said, her eyes back to the doorway in time to see Marci storm off, Don scurrying after her.

"He asked me out," Lea revealed in a low voice, even though no one else was nearby.

"Who? Don?"

Lea nodded, her bangs flying up, then dropping back in place on her forehead.

"Just now?" Deena's delicate mouth formed an O of surprise.

"Yes. Just now. He asked me out just now." Lea had to laugh at her new friend's astonished expression.

Deena reached across the table and tapped the back of Lea's hand with one finger. "Watch out for Marci," she warned.

"Deena, come on, I'm sure Don—"

"Just watch out for her," Deena repeated seriously.

Lea twisted around to check out the lunchroom doorway. Several kids were leaving. The lunchroom was clearing out. It was just about time for the bell for fifth period to ring.

"What did you spill on her?" Deena asked, sliding her chair back and standing up.

"Chili," Lea said, starting to feel embarrassed all over again.

"On that white cashmere sweater she was wearing?"

"It was *cashmere?*" Lea cried, horrified.

To Lea's surprise, Deena was laughing.

"It's not funny," Lea said. "I was mortified!"

"It is funny—if you know Marci" was Deena's explanation.

They walked to their lockers, Deena still chuckling and shaking her head, Lea thinking about Don, wondering why he had asked her out if he and Marci had been a couple for so long.

"See you later," Deena said, heading down the hall to her class.

But Lea didn't hear her. She was thinking about Marci and Deena's warning to watch out for her, and she was wondering if she hadn't already made an enemy, on this, her second week in school.

chapter

2

Lea's house loomed in front of her like some dark monster in a horror movie. It's just as old and creepy in the afternoon as it is at night, Lea realized, shifting her backpack from one shoulder to the other and starting up the broken flagstone walk to the front door.

Above her, two windows on the second floor, her bedroom windows, caught the glow of the late-afternoon sun and seemed to light up. Like two evil eyes, she thought.

The house sees me coming home to it after school and opens its eyes. And now I'm about to step into its gaping, dark mouth.

Chill out, Lea, she scolded herself. Let's not be overly dramatic.

So the house is big and ramshackle and a wreck. That doesn't make it evil.

Even if it is on Fear Street.

She unlocked the front door, struggling with the still-unfamiliar lock, and stepped into the dark front hallway. It was warm in the house despite the cool autumn air outside, warm and damp, with that sour, musty smell some old houses have.

Why on earth do Mom and Dad have to like these old places? she asked herself, the floorboards creaking under her feet as she tossed her backpack down and made her way through the empty house to the kitchen to get a snack.

Sitting at the table in the small breakfast alcove, the flowered wallpaper stained and peeling, Lea spooned blueberry yogurt from the container into a bowl and thought about the first time she had seen the house, less than a month earlier.

It had been an afternoon much like this one, cool, breezy, the feel of autumn in the air despite the bright yellow sun high in the sky. The light, it had seemed to Lea, was cut off as soon as the real estate agent led them into the house, closing the front door behind her. It was as if someone had turned off a bright flashlight, Lea remembered, as if the house was turning away the sunlight, shutting it out, covering them in its warm darkness.

She had immediately been appalled by the age-stained walls, the dust-blanketed windows, the warped moldings, the threadbare, old carpets covering the creaking floors. The smell of it. The feel of it.

Her parents, of course, had immediately fallen in love with it.

"It's charming," Mr. Carson had said.

"Think of all we can do here," Mrs. Carson had replied.

Mrs. Thomas, the real estate agent, a pleasant-looking woman wearing a very smart tweed suit and a permanent smile, caught the unhappy expression on Lea's face.

"Let me show you the bedrooms upstairs," she said, turning her smile on Lea. "They need work, of course. But they're very large. The second bedroom—I suppose that will be your room, Lea—is the brightest room in the house. The two windows face the front, and sunlight streams in all day long."

"It's so dark in the living room," Lea said gloomily. She wanted to beg her parents not to take this house, but she knew it was hopeless. They had lived in three different houses in the past seven years, all of them as run-down and creepy looking as this one.

"It won't be dark after I install track lighting," Mr. Carson said, eyeing the living-room ceiling, then checking out the electrical outlets along the molding by the floor.

"Come on upstairs," Mrs. Thomas said to Lea. "Be careful. The banister may be loose."

Lea followed her up the stairs, which swayed under their weight and seemed to groan in protest with each stair they stepped on. "The banister is easy to fix," Mr. Carson said cheerily.

"I'd like to carpet the stairway," Lea's mother said. "And continue the carpeting down the landing here. Something light. It'll brighten up everything, make it look new."

"Yeah, sure," Lea muttered under her breath, knowing they would hear her, hoping they realized how unhappy she was.

She was unhappy about moving to Shadyside in the first place. It had taken her so long to make friends back in Daly City, to feel comfortable and happy there. And just when she was starting to have a good time, her dad got transferred again and she'd have to start a new school four weeks after the term began.

"Wow, Lea, look how big your room is," her mother exclaimed as they stepped into the big, square room. The two windows on the far wall glowed with yellow sunlight. Squares of warm light stretched across the worn blue carpeting.

"See? I was right about the light," Mrs. Thomas said, her hands in her jacket pockets, her smile solidly in place. "And take a look at the closet, Lea."

Lea obediently walked over to the closet.

"We'll pull up your carpeting first thing," Lea's father said. "And we'll sand the floors."

Lea pulled open the closet door and stared into the vast, black cavern behind it. She had a sudden chill. *It's like a cave, an animal's den,* she thought. *What kind of creature is lurking in this dark cave?*

"Did you ever see such a big walk-in closet?" Mrs. Thomas asked triumphantly, coming up behind Lea and gently resting a hand on her shoulder. Mrs. Thomas smelled of peppermint. Lea inhaled deeply. It was such a sweet fragrance in the sour, old house.

"It's really big," Lea said, peering in, her eyes adjusting to the darkness. "It's as big as a room."

Mrs. Thomas seemed very pleased by Lea's reaction. "Lots of closet space," she said. "Are you a senior this year, Lea?"

"No. A junior."

"My daughter, Suki, goes to Shadyside. She's a senior. I'll tell her to come over and say hi to you."

"Thanks, Mrs. Thomas," Lea said awkwardly.

"Now, let me show you the rest of the second floor," Mrs. Thomas said, turning her attention back to Lea's parents. "There's a charming extra room that could be a guest bedroom or a study."

Taking a last look at what would soon become her room, Lea followed them out into the hallway. Mrs. Thomas and her parents were nearly to the end of the dark corridor. She could hear Mrs. Thomas chattering enthusiastically about the possibilities for the master bedroom.

"Hey—what's this?" Lea had stopped at a metal ladder bolted into the wall just outside her bedroom door. Peering up, she saw that it led to a wooden trapdoor in the ceiling. "Where does this go?" Lea asked.

The three adults came back to where Lea was standing. Mr. Carson tested the metal ladder for sturdiness. "Must lead up to the attic," he said, staring up at the ceiling trapdoor.

"Yes, there's an attic up there," Mrs. Thomas said, checking the notes on her clipboard. "Quite a sizable one, actually. Want to see it?"

"No, thanks," Lea said immediately.

"Of course," Mrs. Carson said. "I love attics. When I was a little girl, I spent all my time up in our attic, playing with all the treasures up there."

"Yeah. Treasures," Lea said sarcastically. "Like spiders and dirt and bats."

Mrs. Carson gave Lea an unhappy look. "I really wish you'd make an effort."

"To do what?" Lea snapped.

"To get into this more," her mother said. "To be more cheerful. At least a little bit. It's hard for *all* of us, you know. Not just you."

Lea felt embarrassed. Mrs. Thomas was staring at her. She hated to be scolded in front of strangers. Why couldn't her mother ever learn?

"Okay. Wow! Let's check out the attic," she said with false enthusiasm. She moved in front of her dad, bumping him out of the way, grabbed the sides of the gray metal ladder, and began to climb.

"I think you just push the door away," Mrs. Thomas called up to her. "Just slide it off the opening."

Lea reached up to the ceiling and pushed against the trapdoor with both hands. It lifted easily. She slid it off the opening and climbed a few more rungs on the ladder until her head poked into the attic.

It was hot up there, at least ten degrees hotter than in the house. The attic, Lea saw, was all one open space, long and low. The ceiling followed the slant of the roof just above it. The walls were plasterboard, cracked and yellowing. A single round window at one end lit the entire area.

"Climb on up so we can see it too," her father called impatiently.

Lea pulled herself up into the room. When she stood up, there were only a couple of inches to spare above her head. Her father, who was six-three, would have to stoop.

"It's so beautiful up here!" she called down to them, her voice dripping with sarcasm. "I want to spend all my time up here, with all of the wonderful treasures."

"Lea, give us a break," her father said, pulling his large frame through the narrow opening, then standing up as best as he could to check out the attic.

A few seconds later Lea's mom and Mrs. Thomas joined them in the low, stuffy space. "Not much air up here," Mrs. Carson said, fanning herself with her hand, her first complaint of the day.

"This will make a wonderful storage area," Mrs. Thomas said, scratching the back of her neck.

This place makes *me* itch too, Lea thought bitterly.

Lea walked to the small, round window. Through the dust-caked glass, she could see down to the driveway and a small corner of the front yard, overgrown with weeds and tall grass. The afternoon sun was lowering behind the trees.

Then she walked past the three adults to the wall on the opposite side of the room. "Hey—what's this door?" she called, her voice louder than she had intended in the closed-in space.

A wooden door in the wall had been boarded up with a crisscross of two-by-fours. Lea reached out and tried turning the doorknob. The door was locked. "What's in there? Why is this door boarded up?" Lea asked.

The others joined her. Mr. Carson turned the knob, coming to the same conclusion Lea had. It was locked.

He inspected the two-by-fours. "Looks like someone boarded up this room a long time ago," he said, knocking hard on the door. It sounded thick and solid.

Mrs. Thomas gripped her clipboard and held it tightly against her chest. The smile faded from her face for the first time that afternoon. "Well, that door is a very interesting story," she said, a little reluctantly. And then she quickly added, "I always think that mysterious stories add to the charm of a house—don't you?"

Lea felt a sudden stab of dread. She felt closed in. The walls seemed to be moving in on her, the ceiling lowering. She took a deep breath, her eyes examining the locked, boarded-up door.

Lea's parents exchanged glances. Mr. Carson leaned back against the wall, his head bent down because of the low ceiling.

"What *kind* of mysterious story?" Mrs. Carson asked, her dark eyes alive with interest.

Mrs. Thomas continued to press the clipboard tightly against the front of her jacket. "Of course, most of the houses on Fear Street have similar stories," she started, speaking softly. "They're not true, I don't think. At least, they're not *all* true."

She stared straight ahead at the brass doorknob.

"You mean it's some kind of horror story?" Mrs. Carson asked, even more intrigued.

Lea shifted her weight uncomfortably.

"I don't really know the details," Mrs. Thomas said. "You know how these stories get lost or exaggerated over time. All I know is that there is a room on the other side of that door. And something terrible happened in that room."

"Something—terrible?" Lea asked.

"It was a hundred years ago. At least a hundred years," Mrs. Thomas said, her face covered in shadow as the light through the attic window faded. "And someone was murdered in that room. At least, that's how the story goes."

"You don't know who? Or why?" Lea asked, staring at the two-by-fours that blocked the doorway.

Mrs. Thomas shook her head. "A murder. That's all I know. And the room . . . it's been locked and boarded up ever since."

A hush fell as all four occupants stared silently at the wooden door.

Mrs. Carson broke the silence with a cough. "We'll leave it just the way it is," she said, looking at Lea's dad as if for reassurance.

"Aren't you curious about what's behind it?" Mr. Carson asked. He hunched forward and knocked on the door again. "Hello in there. Anybody home?" he called loudly.

They all listened as if expecting a reply. Then they laughed. Nervous laughter.

"No. I don't want to touch this door," Mrs. Carson said firmly. "We've got more than enough to do downstairs."

That's for sure, Lea thought glumly.

"People make up these stories," Mrs. Thomas said, brightening. "I don't know why. As I said, there's a horror story for every house on Fear Street. Yet the people I've met who live on this street are all as nice as can be."

She edged herself back to the trapdoor and, with difficulty, holding the clipboard in one hand, began to lower herself down the ladder. "Come on, folks. There are some features in the kitchen I didn't get a chance to show you."

Her parents disappeared down the ladder, but Lea lingered behind. She stared at the door, drawn to it and repelled by it at the same time.

Did a murder really take place in this house? In this attic? In the room behind the door?

And even if a murder had taken place there, why was the room locked and boarded up—for a hundred years?

Lea moved closer, closer, until she was standing right in front of the door. She pressed her open palms against the wood.

She felt a chill despite the heat of the attic.

On a sudden impulse she pressed her ear against the door.

"Oh!"

What was that sound she heard?

What *was* it?

Was it *breathing*?

No.

No, no, no.

No, the sound was that of her own breathing. Was she really breathing so hard?

She stepped away from the door, feeling foolish.

It was my own breathing, she told herself.

There were no sounds from the other side of the door.

I wonder what the room on the other side looks like, she thought, drawn to the door once again, feeling its mysterious pull.

No.

I've got to get downstairs now.

She forced herself to turn around, to turn away from it. Still hearing her own rapid, fluttery breathing, she lowered herself down through the narrow, rectangular opening, carefully replacing the trapdoor in the ceiling.

chapter

3

"Y es, I know. He'll be here any minute," Lea said. Without realizing it, she had wrapped the phone cord round and round her wrist, and now she was having trouble untangling it.

"I seem to be tangled up," she told Deena, holding the phone between her shoulder and her chin and using her free hand to remove the cord. "No, I'm not nervous or anything," Lea said, laughing.

Just because it's eight o'clock on Saturday night and I have a date with one of the most popular seniors at school—why should I be nervous? Lea thought.

She pulled the phone as far as it would go so that she could take another look at her hair in the oval mirror above her dresser. Maybe I should get rid of these stupid bangs, she thought. I've had them since I was ten. Everyone is always telling me how *cute* they are.

Maybe I don't want to be *cute* anymore. Maybe I want to be sophisticated now.

Maybe I need a whole new look. Maybe I'll wear my hair spiky, get long, dangly earrings— Right! And maybe I'll grow six inches so everyone won't think I look like some sort of pixie.

So *cute* . . .

"What, Deena? I'm sorry. I wasn't listening," Lea admitted. Deena chattered excitedly in Lea's ear while Lea pulled at her sweater, rearranging the collar. "Yeah. Sure. I'll call you tomorrow morning. Promise."

Lea realized she had the phone cord twisted around her wrist again. I've got to calm down, she told herself. I'll be a nervous wreck by the time Don gets here.

Licking her lips, she glanced at her desk clock for the thousandth time. Eight-ten. "What, Deena? What are you doing tonight?"

Deena's friend Jade Smith was coming over, and they were going to do each other's hair.

"Oh, wait. I think I hear the doorbell," Lea said excitedly. She held the receiver away from her ear and listened.

Was she hearing things?

"No. No, it wasn't," she told her friend. "This old house makes so many noises. Yeah. I know. Listen, Deena, I'd better get off the phone. Yeah. I'm hearing bells. Talk to you tomorrow, okay? Say hi to Jade for me. No—don't cut your hair. I think you should let it grow. Yeah. Okay. Bye."

She replaced the receiver, which was wet from her sweaty hand. Picking up a bath towel she had tossed onto her bed, Lea dried her clammy hands, listening for the bell.

She paced back and forth for a while, catching glimpses of herself in the oval mirror as she passed. The desk clock read eight twenty-three.

Where is he?

She sat down on the edge of her bed, tossing the bath towel to the floor, and picked up Georgie, the stuffed tiger she'd had since she was a baby, her special stuffed animal. She squeezed the tiger tightly, hugging him to her chest.

"What am I doing?" she asked herself aloud.

She tossed the worn, old tiger gently onto her pillow and picked up a copy of *Sassy* magazine. An article called "Twenty Intriguing Things To Say on a First Date" caught her eye. She started to read it, but because of her nervousness, the words blurred until they were just black blotches on the page.

She tried flipping through the magazine, just scanning the pictures, but she didn't have the patience or concentration for that, either.

Lea tossed the magazine across the bed, sighed loudly, and climbed to her feet, uncertain what to do next.

"Lea?"

Her mother's voice startled her from the bottom of the stairs.

"Lea?"

"Yes, Mom?" Lea shouted from her doorway.

"Aren't you going out tonight?" her mother called.

Lea wanted to murder her! "Mom—I've told you a thousand times I'm going out tonight!" she shouted angrily. "What's the matter with you, anyway?"

Whoa, Lea warned herself.

Don't take it out on Mom just because you're nervous about Don.

"He's a little late, I guess," Lea called down in a softer tone.

Her mother didn't reply. Lea could hear her walk away from the stairway, could hear her shoes scrape against the floor, hear the old floorboards creak and squeak.

She turned to check the clock once more. Eight thirty-two.

"I'll call his house," she said aloud.

She took a deep breath. But I don't know his number, she thought.

She crept downstairs to get the phone book from the front hall closet. She didn't want her mom or dad to see her because then she'd have to explain that she was calling Don's house to see why he was late. And that would just be too embarrassing.

Phone book under her arm, she hurried back up the stairs, the wooden steps groaning annoyingly as she climbed.

A few seconds later she found the number. Her heart was racing as she punched it in and listened. One ring. Two.

"Hello?" A woman's voice. Most likely Don's mother.

"Hi. Is Don there?"

A brief pause. "No, he isn't. Who is this?"

"Oh. This is Lea."

"Lea?"

There was loud crackling on the line. "Lea Carson," Lea said loudly, trying to be heard over the static. "I'm sorry to bother you. Don was supposed to pick me up at eight and—"

"But Don's out with Marci," the woman interrupted, sounding very confused.

"What?"

"He left about an hour ago, dear."

"But that's *impossible!*" Lea cried. Then she immediately felt embarrassed.

"Are you sure you have the right number?" Don's mother asked.

"No. I—uh—guess not. Sorry," Lea said. She hung up quickly.

The room seemed to close in on her. The antique mahogany dresser, the rolltop desk that had been her father's, the half-empty bookshelf, the cartons stacked against the wall that she hadn't had time to unpack. They were all sliding toward the bed, surrounding her in a tighter and tighter circle.

She closed her eyes.

When she opened them, everything was back in place.

Don's mother must be mistaken, Lea thought.

Maybe Don told her he was going out with Marci because he didn't want to go into any lengthy explanation about me.

Yes. That must be it.

But—where *is* he?

The clock dial seemed to throb, glowing brighter and brighter until she had to force herself to tear her eyes away from it. Eight forty-seven.

24

I'm not going to sit around here and drive myself crazy, Lea decided.

Without really thinking about it, she opened the Shadyside phone book. Her trembling finger rapidly ran through the H's.

"Hendryx, three-forty-two Canyon Road," Lea read aloud.

Sitting stiffly on the edge of the bed and leaning over the small night table that held the phone, she punched in the number quickly before she could change her mind.

Someone picked up before the first ring had ended. "Hello?"

Lea recognized Marci's voice at once.

"Marci? It's Lea Carson."

"I don't believe it," Marci said, not into the phone but to someone else at her house. "Lea?" she said into the phone.

"Marci—is—uh . . ."

Why did I call her? Lea moaned to herself. This is so embarrassing. I'll never live this down. Never!

"Marci, is Don there?"

Marci's laughter burst into Lea's ear, cold and cruel.

"Marci—?"

Marci stopped laughing abruptly. "Lea, I can't believe you fell for it," she said with false hilarity.

"What?"

"You didn't really believe Don would go out with you, did you?" Marci continued. "It was a *joke.*"

"Now, wait a minute—" Lea could feel her anger rising, replacing her embarrassment.

"No, *you* wait a minute!" Marci snapped angrily.

"Why on earth would Don go out with you? He's going with *me*. It was all a joke, Lea. I dared him to ask you out. But I never *dreamed* you'd fall for it."

Marci held her hand over the mouthpiece. Lea could hear her muffled voice saying something to someone else. Probably Don.

"Well, that will teach you to come on to *my* boyfriend," Marci said nastily. "Have a nice night." The phone clicked loudly in Lea's ear.

Lea slammed down the receiver. Then with a cry of anger, she fell forward on the bed, burying her face in the pillow.

This isn't happening, she thought.

She pressed her face into the soft darkness of the pillow and stifled the urge to scream again.

To scream and scream and scream.

What good would it do? she asked herself. It would only bring her parents. And she definitely didn't want to see her parents.

She didn't want to see *anyone*.

Ever again.

I'll run away, she thought.

I'll take the car. I'll drive and drive and drive—till I fall off the earth!

No. I'll drive and drive and drive—till I run over Marci!

Realizing that she was suffocating, Lea pulled the pillow away from her face. But she didn't move from her facedown position on the bed.

Marci is such a liar, she thought.

Liar, liar, liar.

It wasn't a joke when Don asked me out in the lunchroom. He meant it. He really wanted to go out with me.

Marci forced him to do this.

Yes, that's it.

Marci found out about it and forced him to break the date. Of course. And now she was lying, saying it was all a joke, that she had planned the whole thing, that it was just a stupid dare.

For sure!

It wasn't a joke. Don is much too nice a guy to do something like that. Much too nice . . .

Lea thought about how cute Don had looked down on the floor, helping her pick up her lunch. She thought about Don's shy smile when he asked her out. How nervous he suddenly became, how his eyes kept darting to the lunchroom door.

No, it wasn't a joke.

Marci had forced Don to do this.

Liar, liar, liar.

But then, if that was true, why hadn't Don called her? He could've called and explained. Or made an excuse. Any excuse.

Why had he gone along with Marci's cruel joke?

Was he afraid of Marci? Or—was he just as cruel as she was?

No!

Confused and angry, feeling terribly sorry for herself, Lea picked up her stuffed tiger and clutched it tightly under her chin. "You would never betray

27

me, would you, Georgie?" she asked it in a tiny voice.

Sighing loudly, Lea kicked off the covers. She couldn't get to sleep. She'd been trying for the longest time.

She pulled herself up onto her elbows and stared across the room at the windows. Curtains hadn't been put up yet, and silver moonlight filled both windows. The light was pale and lovely and made the rest of the room shimmer.

I'll never sleep again, Lea thought. She thought about Don and Marci and wondered where they were right then, wondered if they were still talking about her, still laughing at her expense.

I've got to stop thinking about them, she told herself. But that was easier said than done.

The creaking sound brought Lea out of her unhappy thoughts.

She listened as the sound repeated. It seemed to be right over her head.

There it was again.

It wasn't just the creaking of the house. Lea was beginning to recognize the groans and squeaks the old house made.

This sound was too regular, too rhythmic.

She lay back on her pillow, alert now, listening harder.

There the noise was again.

Footsteps?

Yes. It sounded like footsteps up above her.

But that was impossible.

Hugging Georgie, she listened intently.

The sound faded and died.

Her imagination was playing tricks on her.

Tricks . . . tricks . . . tricks . . .

Just a joke . . . just a trick . . . trick . . . trick . . .

With the word repeating in her mind, Lea drifted into a troubled, restless sleep.

chapter
4

Deena, where are you? Lea thought impatiently, leaning against the tile in the hall outside the lunchroom. They had agreed to meet for lunch after fourth period on Monday. Kids were streaming past Lea, laughing, talking loudly, eager for lunch, but Deena was nowhere to be seen.

As she watched everyone go past, Lea had to fight the feeling that they all knew. That they all knew the cruel joke that had been played on her, that they knew how foolish she had been, how gullible.

They all know. And they're all laughing at me.

She avoided everyone's eyes, staring down at her sneakers.

Marci has spread the story all over school. I know she has.

It had taken Lea so much effort just to return to school. She had spent all of Sunday moping around the house, feeling humiliated, betrayed, mortified beyond words. When Deena had called Sunday afternoon wondering why she hadn't heard from Lea, the whole story had burst out of Lea in a stream of anger.

Deena had tried to be comforting. But Lea detected a tone of "I told you so" in Deena's voice, which made Lea feel even more foolish and alone.

And now, here she was, standing by the door to the lunchroom with the whole school marching by, everyone staring at her, everyone grinning.

Everyone knows.

Lea scolded herself for being paranoid, but she still avoided everyone's glance.

Suddenly someone bumped into her shoulder, hard. "Hey—" she cried out.

"Sorry. He pushed me." A chubby guy with dark, curly hair grinned at her while pointing at a kid beside him. She recognized him from her homeroom. His name was Ricky Schorr, and he was always goofing around. He shoved his friend back, and they continued on into the lunchroom, carrying on like little kids.

Everyone here is so immature, Lea thought glumly.

Except for me. I'm not mature enough to be immature.

She was about to give up on Deena when a voice interrupted her thoughts. "Hi, Lea."

Lea swung around to see Don standing next to her, guilt written across his face. "Hi," she said coldly, forcing herself not to act surprised to see him there, forcing herself not to reveal any emotion at all.

"I—I don't know what to say," Don muttered,

staring into her eyes. He had his hands stuffed in his jeans pockets. He rocked uncomfortably back and forth on his sneakers.

Lea didn't reply.

He continued to stare into her eyes. "I just want to—you know, apologize."

Lea glanced down the long hall, which had emptied out except for a few stragglers. She didn't say anything.

"I wanted to call you, to let you know," Don said, removing one hand from a pocket to rub the back of his neck. "Marci—well, she's sort of jealous. I mean—"

He stopped, hoping she'd say something, hoping she'd help him out.

But Lea didn't say a word.

She turned her glance on him, leaving her face expressionless. He had beads of perspiration on his forehead even though it was cold in the hall.

"Marci's great, really," Don continued, still rocking up and down on his sneakers. "You've only seen the bad side of her. She just gets really jealous, that's all."

He stopped, took a deep breath, and let it out, shaking his head. "I shouldn't be apologizing for her," he said, staring at Lea's face. "I should be apologizing for me. I'm really sorry, Lea."

"Thanks for apologizing, Don," she said, keeping her voice low and steady.

"Last week in the lunchroom," he continued, a little less awkwardly. "When I saw you, I thought—" He stopped suddenly. Lea followed his gaze down the hall.

Marci had just turned the corner.

Lea felt a sharp stab of anger, mixed with dread.

"Uh—I'd better go," Don said quickly. "Sorry. Really. I really am." He turned and, dodging two girls on their way to the lunchroom, hurried in a half run to intercept Marci.

Lea remained against the wall, unmoving, watching Don and Marci. He caught up to her, took her by the arm, and turned her around. They disappeared back around the corner.

Wow, thought Lea. Marci sure does have Don wrapped around her little finger!

"Sorry I'm late," Deena said, appearing from behind Lea, grabbing Lea's shoulder.

Lea, lost in thought, jumped in surprise. "Oh, hi."

"Wagner kept me after class. I totally blew the chem experiment. He wouldn't let me leave till I got it right."

"Oh, that's okay," Lea said wistfully, following her friend into the lunchroom. "I'm not very hungry, anyway."

"You still thinking about Don and Marci?" Deena asked sympathetically.

"Yeah. I guess." Lea shrugged. "I wish I could just shut them out of my mind. Just shut the door on them, lock it, and board it up—like the room in my attic."

"The room in your attic?" Deena was totally mystified.

"Never mind," Lea said, and picked up a lunch tray from the stack, burning hot and soaking wet, as usual.

* * *

After school Lea pulled some books out of her locker, loaded her backpack, closed the locker, and prepared to lock it. It was then she realized that Marci was standing beside her.

Marci's short red hair was perfectly brushed, and she was wearing a very short green suede skirt over black tights and a silky green top that emphasized her full figure. Just standing next to her made Lea feel small and boyish.

"Marci, what do you want?" Lea asked, sounding more impatient than angry.

"I want to apologize too," Marci said softly.

"What?" Lea hoisted the backpack onto her shoulders.

"I made Don apologize, and now I want to apologize too."

Lea had the sudden feeling that she was in a dream, that she was sound asleep, fashioning this whole scene from her subconscious. She stared past Marci down the hall. The solid walls, the bright ceiling lights, the other kids at their lockers, all seemed to indicate that this wasn't a dream. It was really happening.

"You *made* Don apologize?" Lea couldn't hide her surprise or her confusion.

"I went too far," Marci said, staring into Lea's eyes. "I really did. I'm not a mean person. Usually. And this time I just went too far. After Saturday I felt terrible."

"So did I," Lea said bitterly.

"I want to make it up to you," Marci said, putting a hand briefly on Lea's shoulder. "We're having a sorority meeting tomorrow after school. Would you like to come see if you'd be interested in joining?"

Lea stared into Marci's eyes, trying to read her thoughts.

Was she sincere? Was she really inviting Lea to join her sorority? To become part of her group?

Lea had always wanted to belong, really belong, but wherever she went, she had always been the outsider, the shy outsider.

"I—I didn't know there were sororities at Shadyside," Lea stammered.

"Of course there are." Marci smiled. "We're meeting after school tomorrow in Room four-oh-nine. Please come, Lea." She held Lea's shoulder again briefly. "I really would like to make it up to you for last weekend. I just feel so guilty."

Lea pulled away from Marci angrily. "Hey, I'm not stupid!" she snapped, glaring at her. "This school is only three stories high. There *is* no Room four-oh-nine!"

Marci threw back her head and laughed. *"Never mind!"* she cried in a mocking voice. She turned and hurried away, still laughing to herself.

"What a dumb joke," Lea tried to call after her, but her voice choked in her throat, and the words didn't come out.

Lea slammed her fist angrily against her locker. The pain ran up her arm to her shoulder. "Ow."

At least Marci's stupid joke didn't work.

At least Lea was smart enough to remember how many floors there were at Shadyside.

Yeah, I'm real smart, Lea told herself bitterly. Real smart . . .

She checked to make sure she had secured her lock, then glumly began to trudge down the long hall toward the front entrance.

Why does Marci want to *torture* me? she wondered.

Why does she hate me so much?

She can *have* Don. Really. I'm not interested in him. I hope the two of them are very happy.

Let them just leave me alone to live my lonely life.

As she stepped out the door, she raised her eyes to the sky. It was gray and threatening rain, and she felt the gusty autumn wind whip up and sting her face. Looking down at the bottom of the steps, she saw Marci on the sidewalk talking to a cluster of girls.

When Lea stepped off the steps, they instantly stopped talking and glanced over at her. Then they all started to laugh.

Marci was telling them about me, Lea realized.

Anger she had never felt before rose up through her body.

I've got to get back at Marci, Lea thought, frightened by her own vehemence.

I've *got* to get back at her.

chapter
5

*L*ea pushed Stop on the remote control, then pushed Rewind. The VCR clicked obediently and began to rewind the movie.

It was Saturday night and she was home alone, stretched out on the couch in the den, having just watched *Ghost* for the third time in as many months, or maybe the fourth. She had lost track.

Patrick Swayze is a real babe, she thought, stretching sleepily. He can come haunt me anytime.

Yawning, Lea glanced up at the grandfather clock in the corner of the room beside the cartons of unpacked books. "Two-fifteen?"

She had momentarily forgotten that the clock didn't work. It was just another piece of "valuable" junk her dad had bought at a garage sale, intending to fix it when he had the chance.

She smiled, thinking about her dad. In his job as an electronics company recruiter, he did nothing with his hands, except maybe push papers back and forth across a desk. But when he got home, his hands were constantly busy with projects, building, examining, repairing everything, as if they had to make up for all the time they spent in repose during the day.

Her mother, Lea knew, had the same energy, the same drive to fix things up, to make things better, to improve the world by painting it or wallpapering it.

By the time they're finished with this old dump, Lea thought, it'll look like a real home.

But then, of course, it'll be time to move.

When I get married, I'm going to settle into one place and never move, she told herself, smiling at the thought. Maybe I'll just dig a hole in the ground, a soft, comfy hole, just big enough for me and my family, and live in it forever, rooted there like a tree.

She wandered up to her room, turning off lights along the way, making sure the porch light was on for her parents. They were at a party across town being given by a man from her dad's new office. A welcoming party, her dad had described it.

Wish someone would give *me* a welcoming party, Lea thought wistfully.

Her desk clock said it was only eleven-thirty. I don't care how early it is. I'm tired and I'm going to go to sleep, she decided.

The next day, Sunday, she and Deena had made plans to go play tennis at an indoor tennis club Deena's family belonged to in the North Hills section of town.

Something to look forward to, Lea thought, yawning sleepily. She pushed Georgie to the foot of the bed, clicked off the lamp on her night table, and slid under the covers.

Darkness covered her like a soft blanket. Outside the twin windows clouds blocked the moon. The sky was gray and still.

Lea settled her head on the pillow, staring up at the smooth blackness of the ceiling. At least I was able to bring my old bed with me, she thought happily. Something familiar. Something cozy . . .

She had almost drifted into a pleasant sleep when she heard the noise again.

Clearer this time.

Above her head.

Footsteps. It *had* to be footsteps.

But how could it be?

She tried to ignore the sound, shutting her eyes tightly and pulling the soft feather pillow up over her ears.

But she could still hear them.

Footsteps. The ceiling groaned under them.

One step. Then another. Then in the other direction. As if someone was pacing above her head.

Someone upstairs in the attic.

Or some*thing*.

But how could that be? The round attic window was too high and too small for anyone to climb in. And there was no other entryway.

Lea sat up.

The ceiling squeaked directly overhead.

Shoes against the floor above. *Tap. Tap.* Then back—*tap tap.* Louder now.

No!

Lea kicked off the covers and stood up, her heart pounding.

"Hey!" she called out, staring up at the dark ceiling.

She listened.

The tapping stopped for a moment, then started again.

Suddenly very frightened, she clicked on the lamp, then turned on the ceiling light. She pulled her silky blue robe on over her pajamas and slipped into the rubber thongs she used as slippers.

Maybe I should call the police, she thought.

After all, here I am all alone in the house, and someone is definitely walking around up there.

But, of course, there *couldn't* be anyone walking around up there.

And if someone *had* somehow gotten in up there, why was he just pacing back and forth? Why hadn't he made any move to come down?

That's because it's all just my imagination or creepy, old house noises, Lea told herself. Maybe there's a shingle loose on the roof.

Yes. Of course. That has to be it. A loose shingle. And every time the wind blows it, it tilts up, then comes down with a tapping noise.

Lea felt a little better.

But she knew she had to find out for sure.

She was surprised to find herself on the metal ladder outside her bedroom door. It was as if she had sleepwalked out to the hall. And now there she was, climbing the ladder despite the heavy feeling of dread in her chest, climbing the ladder and pushing the trapdoor up and out of the way, and climbing higher, high enough to peer into the long, low attic.

"Anybody up here?" she called, surprised by her own bravery.

The darkness was thick and cold. And silent.

Of *course* there isn't anyone up here, she told herself.

She pulled herself up onto the attic floor, then groped along the wall until she found the light switch. A single bulb suspended from the ceiling cast pale yellow light over the room.

Lea stared at the window, then turned and let her eyes examine the boarded-up room.

Nothing. No one. Silence.

Breathing a soft sigh of relief, she moved to turn off the light.

Then she heard the footsteps again. Clearly.

Very close.

Three steps one way, two steps back.

Lea looked around expectantly, listening, hoping the noise came from above her, from the roof. Hoping her broken shingle theory would prove true.

But she knew at once where the sounds were coming from. They were coming from the room, from behind the locked door.

This is crazy, she thought.

But she moved to the door, taking off her thongs so she could walk even more silently. She leaned against one of the two-by-fours, pressing her ear against the wood.

This is crazy. This is *so* crazy.

She continued to hear the sounds.

Yes. She heard them coming from the other side of the door.

Crazy. Crazy. Crazy.

I must be going crazy.

This room has been locked up for a hundred years. Locked and blockaded for a hundred years.

"Hello! Can you hear me?" she shouted into the door.

She leaned forward expectantly, pressing her ear hard against the old wood.

From the other side she heard nothing now. The sounds had stopped.

Lea's heart was pounding. She tingled all over. The dim yellow light made everything unreal, as if she were living in a faded, old movie.

The sounds had stopped, as if in response to her call.

"Hello!" she called again, cupping her hands around her mouth and shouting against the door.

Silence on the other side.

A heavy silence, as if someone was listening. Listening to her.

And then she heard a soft plopping, a dripping sound.

Lea raised her head just in time to see the dark liquid begin to ooze out from the top of the doorway. It descended rapidly, in a single wave, flowing straight down the front of the door to the floor, splashing at Lea's feet.

Lea screamed and jumped back.

It was a thick, dark liquid. It was blood. A curtain of

blood. Pouring down the door. Forming a dark, widening circle on the floor at her feet.

Holding her hands to her face, unable to take her eyes from the flowing waterfall of blood, she screamed again.

And again.

chapter

6

"Deena, please—hurry!"

Lea had been screaming into the phone without realizing it.

"Just try to calm down," Deena said, sounding very alarmed on the other end of the line. "You sound hysterical, Lea. You're not making any sense."

"Of *course* I'm not making sense!" Lea shrieked, gripping the phone tightly, gasping for breath. "It doesn't make any sense! Please—hurry."

"Okay. I just have to get some shoes on," Deena told her. "I'll be right there. Where are your parents, anyway?"

"I don't know. Someone's house. They didn't leave a number," Lea said breathlessly, staring at the floor in front of her bedroom door, as if expecting the wave of blood to follow her downstairs.

"I hate Fear Street!" Deena exclaimed. "Why do

you have to live on Fear Street? I had a *horrible* experience on Fear Street last year!"

"Come *on*, Deena. I'm all alone here!" Lea pleaded.

"Okay. Bye." The line went dead.

Lea replaced the receiver, still staring at the floor by the doorway. Of course my story doesn't make sense, she thought. How *could* it make sense?

Footsteps in a room that's been boarded up for a hundred years? A waterfall of blood pouring down over a door?

She dropped down onto the edge of her bed, her hand still on the phone receiver.

She listened. The house was silent now. So silent she could hear the soft ticking of her desk clock. So silent she could hear the brush of wind through the leafless old trees in the front yard.

It was quiet up there now. But was the blood still flowing? Was it flooding the attic? Would it soon seep through her ceiling and down onto her bed?

Terrified, she glanced up at the ceiling.

That enormous, circular dark spot around the brass light fixture—had it been there before? Those long, straight cracks in the plaster. She didn't remember seeing them, either.

I've got to get out of here, she thought.

She darted to her closet, swung open the door, and pulled the light chain. Nothing in the closet seemed familiar to her. Were those her clothes hung on the bar, stacked on the shelves, tossed on the floor, piles of socks and underwear, blouses and T-shirts still waiting to be sorted and put away?

Nothing here is mine, she thought, gripped with panic. Nothing in this house is familiar. Nothing in this house is *right*.

Frantically she pulled off her pajamas, kicking them out of her way, and grabbed a pair of jeans and a green, long-sleeved sweater.

Where should I go? Where can I go?

If only Mom and Dad were here.

But what could *they* do about the blood, the pouring blood?

Lea started out of her room, pausing at the doorway, looking both ways down the hall, then realized she was barefoot.

"Where do you think you're going?" she asked herself out loud. Her voice sounded small and frightened in the vast old house. "You're not thinking clearly."

Glancing up to the top of the ladder, she made sure the trapdoor was in place. Yes.

Even in her panic, even as she had run from the blood, run from the attic, pulled herself in a frenzy down the ladder, trembling all over, more frightened than she had ever been in her life, more frightened than she had ever dreamed possible, she had remembered to replace the trapdoor.

To her relief, it remained in place.

And the house remained quiet.

But upstairs—what? What was happening in the attic?

I'll call the police, she decided.

Why hadn't she thought of it before?

Of course. The police.

She ran downstairs, still barefoot, the wooden stairs cold beneath her feet. She turned on all the lights as she hurried back to the kitchen. After she snatched up the receiver of the kitchen phone, she dialed 911.

Lea heard static over the phone line, before the ringing. A few seconds later a man's voice came on the line. "Sergeant Barnett."

"Hello, I—I need help."

"How can I help you?" he asked, sounding concerned.

"I—I mean, there's blood. In my attic," Lea stammered, staring out the kitchen window into the blackness of the night.

"I beg your pardon?"

"Please—come. I have to show you. It's blood. Pouring down. I'm all alone here." Lea realized she wasn't making much sense. But her mind was spinning. The words wouldn't fit together right.

She spun away from the window, staring back into the long hallway leading to the front of the house, expecting to see something or someone standing there.

But the hallway was empty.

I'm really losing it, she thought.

"Please—hurry," she pleaded into the phone.

"I'll send someone right over," the sergeant said. "Give me your name and address."

Lea's mind went blank.

Name and address?

So this was what panic felt like. This was how it

blanked your mind, made you forget everything—everything but your fear.

I've got to get out of here, she thought.

The doorbell rang.

Deena!

Her memory returned. She told the sergeant her name and address.

The doorbell rang again, longer this time, more insistent.

"Let me just make sure I have it right," Sergeant Barnett said.

Lea groaned. "Please—hurry."

The doorbell rang and rang again.

The police sergeant repeated Lea's address. "We'll have a car there in five minutes," he said. "Will you be okay till then?"

"I hope so," Lea said, hanging up and running through the hallway to the front door. She pulled it open just as Deena rang again.

"Lea—you didn't answer the bell. I was so worried!" Deena's blond hair was windblown, tossed wildly around her face. Her wool poncho flapped behind her in the gusting wind.

"Thanks for coming. Come in. Hurry. It's so windy," Lea said, checking up and down the street. Leaves swirled across the lawn in a wild, unending dance. The old trees bent and swayed. It seemed to her as if the entire front yard had come alive.

Shivering, she slammed the front door. "I-I'm so scared," she said.

"I don't really understand," Deena said, yanking off

her poncho and tossing it onto the banister. "You went up to the attic and saw blood?"

"I was in my room," Lea explained again. "Asleep. But I woke up because I heard noises upstairs."

"Upstairs in the attic?"

"Yes," Lea told her. "Footsteps. At least, it sounded like footsteps. But I knew that was impossible. So I went up to the attic and—and the door—blood started to pour down the door, and—"

Deena was listening to all this openmouthed, her eyes wide with disbelief. Suddenly her expression changed, and she stared intently at Lea.

"Lea, it was a dream," Deena said softly. She reached out and placed her hands gently on Lea's trembling shoulders.

"What?"

"It was a dream. It *had* to be. You were asleep, right? And you dreamed the rest. And then you woke up in your room, thinking it was real. And you called me."

Lea backed out of her friend's hands. "You think I'm cracking up, huh?"

"No, of course not," Deena said patiently. "Some dreams can be really vivid. I have very real dreams too."

"It wasn't a dream," Lea insisted angrily. "The blood poured right down to my feet."

Deena glanced down at Lea's bare feet. "Did you wash it off?"

"No, of course not. I didn't have time," Lea replied, glancing down at her feet too.

There were no bloodstains on her feet. Not a trace.

She lifted her head up. "I jumped back. I got out of the way of the blood. Then I ran downstairs."

"Lea—" Deena started. But Lea grabbed her friend's hand and pulled her to the stairway. "Hey—what are you doing?"

"I'll show you," Lea said. Deena's hand was still cold from the outside. "Come on. I'll show you it wasn't a dream."

"But, Lea, wait—" Deena held back. "Maybe we shouldn't go up there."

"Why are you so frightened if it was only a dream?" Lea asked, challenging her friend.

"I just—" Deena shook her head as if trying to get her thoughts straight. "I don't like dark, old attics."

"Listen," Lea said, tugging at Deena, "you said I was crazy, so—"

"I did *not* say you were crazy. I just said it all sounded like a dream. Like you were having a nightmare."

"It's a nightmare, all right," Lea said, sighing. "But it's real, Deena. It's all real. Come on." She pulled with renewed strength.

"Okay, okay. Don't pull me," Deena said. "I can't believe I'm doing this."

They hesitated at the ladder next to Lea's room. They both stared up at the trapdoor and listened.

Silence.

"Come on," Lea said, whispering. She started up the ladder. "I'll just show you the blood. Then we'll close it up again."

"I really don't like this." Deena stepped onto the ladder, staying close behind Lea.

Lea slid the trapdoor up and away. They both stared up into the silent darkness.

"That's funny," Lea said, glancing down at her friend, bewildered. "I left the attic light on. I'm *sure* I didn't turn it off."

Deena stared back at her, didn't say anything. Then finally she said, "Maybe we should get a flashlight or something."

"No. I'll just turn on the light," Lea said, and disappeared up through the rectangular opening in the ceiling.

"Lea, please—" Deena called softly, her trembling voice revealing her fear. "Don't go. Don't!"

It was too late. Lea had stepped onto the attic floor, and Deena was pulling herself up behind her.

The rough wood of the attic floor felt cold beneath Lea's bare feet. She groped around, found the light switch, and turned it on. The long, narrow attic filled with yellow light.

"There—" Lea said, pointing. "There's the door. And look—"

Both girls huddled together, peering across the attic through the dim yellow light.

Neither of them spoke.

Neither of them moved.

Above their heads the wind was a roar against the roof.

Lea was the first to break the silence. "I don't believe it," she said, her hands pressed tightly against her face.

chapter

7

"No blood," Deena said softly.

"No blood," Lea repeated. The yellow light made everything unreal, dreamlike. But it was easy to see that the door was as it had always been, solid, locked, boarded up—and dry.

"So it was a dream after all," Lea whispered, staring straight ahead.

"What a relief," Deena said, sighing.

Lea knew she should feel relieved. But to her surprise, she felt more frightened than ever. "Let's go downstairs," she said quickly.

Deena led the way down so Lea could replace the trapdoor. They were heading down the stairs when the doorbell rang.

"Police!" a voice called from outside the front door.

"Oh, no!" Lea groaned, raising her hand to her forehead. "I forgot. I called the police. What am I going to tell him?"

"Police!" the voice repeated. This was followed by loud pounding on the door.

"I don't know!" Deena cried.

"I can't tell him I had a bad dream!" Lea wailed.

She pulled open the front door. A very young-looking police officer stood under the porch light in a dark blue uniform, one hand on his gun holster, one hand raised, ready to knock again.

"I'm Officer Beard," he said, his eyes studying first Lea, then Deena. "What's the trouble here?"

"Uh—it's okay, actually," Lea said, holding the storm door open just a few inches.

"Okay?" His small, dark eyes narrowed in suspicion.

"Uh—yeah," Lea said, unable to conceal her embarrassment. "I heard noises up in the attic. I mean, I *thought* I heard noises. But I didn't."

"What *did* you hear?" the police officer asked, relaxing and allowing his hand to slide off the holster and down his side.

"I didn't hear anything. I mean—" Lea turned to Deena for help, but Deena only shrugged. "I went up to the attic. There was nothing there," Lea continued.

"I got a three-oh-two call. Emergency," Officer Beard said, staring into Lea's eyes as if searching for the true story there. "Mind if I come in and have a look around?"

"No. I don't mind," Lea said reluctantly. "But everything is okay. Really."

Lea held the door as the wary police officer came in. Then she followed him around as he made a quick survey of the house.

"Glad there's no problem," he said without smiling, returning to the front door after his search.

"I'm sorry," Lea told him sincerely. "I was scared. I was all alone here. I thought I heard something. I'm really sorry."

"Don't be," the officer said, stepping out onto the front walk and noticing all the empty moving cartons stacked against the side of the house. "This can be a scary neighborhood sometimes. You just move in?"

"Yes." Lea nodded.

"Don't hesitate to call. Better safe than sorry. Know what I mean?" Officer Beard grinned, revealing long, crooked front teeth.

"Thanks, Officer," Lea said, relieved. "Thanks a lot."

He reached up and touched the brim of his cap, a real movie-cop gesture. Lea and Deena watched him walk down the drive to his black-and-white patrol car. Then Lea closed the door and started to lock it.

"No. Don't close it. I've got to go," Deena said, checking her watch. "Are you going to be okay?"

"Yeah. Fine," Lea said, yawning. "Now that I know it was all a dream."

"Jade and I went to this horror movie once," Deena said, "where this girl kept having bad dreams, and the dreams started getting more and more horrible, and she couldn't wake up, and she knew if she didn't wake up, she'd be trapped in a dream forever, and the dream would become her life and her life would become a dream. Jade thought t was really neat, but it gave me nightmares for a month."

"Gee, thanks for sharing that with me," Lea said dryly.

They both laughed.

"I'll be okay," Lea said. "Thanks for coming." She hugged Deena. "You're a real friend."

"Go to sleep. And let's forget about tennis tomorrow—you look a wreck," Deena said, pulling on her poncho and heading out the door.

"Thanks, friend."

A few minutes later Lea was tucked into her bed, the covers pulled up to her chin. The heavy cloud cover had parted, and pale silver moonlight floated in through the twin windows. Lea saw the glare of headlights and thought she heard her parents' car pull up the drive, but it was some other car, turning around.

It must be quite a party, she thought. Mom and Dad don't usually stay out this late.

She had just about drifted off to sleep when she heard sounds above her head. Dull thuds. First in one direction, then back in the other.

The thud of shoes against the wooden floor?

No, no, no.

The sounds, this time like fingers on a drum, grew louder.

Lying on her back, Lea reached up and pulled the sides of the pillow up over her ears. Holding tightly to the pillow, which muffled the sounds above her head, she fell asleep.

* * *

"You sure it wasn't just the natural creaking of the house?" her father asked at breakfast, drops of milk from his cereal catching in his mustache.

Lea shook her head and handed her dad a paper napkin from the plastic dispenser on the table. They were sitting in the small breakfast nook, sharp blades of morning sunlight jabbing through the dust-covered windows. "No, I know those sounds already," Lea said, resting her chin on one hand, shielding her eyes from the invading sunlight with the other.

"We've got to get curtains up in here," her mother said, squinting. "Lea, you want to trade places with me? You're looking right into the sun."

"Maybe there's a squirrel or two up there," her father suggested, lifting the cereal bowl to his mouth and tipping it to drink the remaining milk.

"You must've been so scared," her mother said, struggling to remove a section from her grapefruit. "I mean, to have called the police."

"Yeah, it was scary," Lea said thoughtfully.

She had decided not to tell them about the blood pouring down the door. Mainly since there *was* no blood pouring down the door. Bad enough that Deena thought she was cracking up. She didn't want to get her parents all worried too.

"Could be squirrels. Or even a raccoon," her father said, sipping his coffee. When he pulled the cup away, his mustache was soaked from it.

How can he stand that mustache? Lea wondered, watching him dab at it with the paper napkin.

"How could a raccoon get in there?" Lea asked.

"They're crafty," her father replied. "They can get in anywhere they want. You ever look carefully at a raccoon's paws?"

"No," Lea said, laughing.

"They're unbelievably dexterous." He curled his big hand up and moved the fingers, a demonstration of a raccoon paw.

"Maybe it *was* a raccoon," Lea said, taking a sip of orange juice. "Yuck. Pulp." She made a sour face.

"I'm sorry," her mother said quickly. "I know you hate pulp. I couldn't find the kind you like. The supermarket is different here."

"That's okay," Lea said. She gingerly took another sip.

"I'll take a look up there later," Mr. Carson said. "But from now on, if you hear noises, just ignore 'em, okay?" He smiled at her, his eyes dark above the red-brown mustache. "Don't panic. That's our motto, right?"

"Right," Lea said, picturing the blood pouring down the door again.

What a dream!

"Time to get a move on," her mother declared, glancing at the stove clock. "We're working on the downstairs bathroom today." Both of Lea's parents jumped up and hurried from the room.

Lea lingered at the table, scooting her chair over to get out of the sunlight. "Don't panic," she said out loud, mimicking her father.

"Easy for him to say."

* * *

57

That night, hunched over her desk, making her way slowly through an endless chapter in her government text, Lea ignored the scraping, tapping sounds above her head.

The following night, lying in bed, thinking about Don Jacobs despite all her best intentions not to think about him, she forced herself to ignore the sounds again.

Thump thump thump. Then back in the opposite direction: *thump thump thump.*

Mr. Carson went up to the attic as he had promised and came back down with nothing to report. "I saw a few dust bunnies up there," he said, smiling. "Maybe we've got very noisy dust bunnies."

"But I heard the sounds again last night," Lea protested. "Loud. Like drumbeats. Or footsteps."

Her father scratched his head, wrinkling his face in thought. "Could be a loose shingle. I'm going to have the roof checked in a week or so."

Lea buried herself in her homework, trying to concentrate the sounds away. Late at night, lying in bed, watching the dim moonlight filter in through the new curtains her mother had just put up, she thought she heard a voice up there, someone talking in a low tone right above her head.

Just ignore it, she instructed herself, and the sound did immediately disappear.

The next night she dreamed about the room above her head.

In the dream she was in bed, unable to sleep because of loud, persistent footsteps on the ceiling. She raised her eyes to the ceiling. The light fixture was shaking.

The whole room began shaking then from the force of the footsteps.

She dreamed that her bed started to slide across the room and she jumped up to run out in the hall in her pajamas. It was very cold in the hallway. She began to climb the ladder to the attic. She felt very afraid, not a daytime fear, but the type that sweeps over you, controls you completely, weakens your muscles, paralyzes your mind—the kind of fear that comes only with a dream.

The attic was dark and cool. When she clicked the light switch, it grew even darker. She crept up to the locked door. At this point Lea knew it was a dream. She wanted to wake up. She *tried* to wake up.

But she couldn't.

She couldn't escape from what was to happen next.

She heard a voice behind the locked door. It was a girl's voice, small and frightened, and sounding very far away.

Lea listened at the door, heard the voice, then started to pull away the heavy boards that blocked the doorway. To her surprise, the boards lifted off easily, as if they were cardboard, and floated away.

Lea hesitated, then placed her hand on the doorknob. It was burning hot!

She screamed and jerked her hand back in pain.

I want to wake up, she thought.

Please—let me out of this dream.

Almost against her will, her hand went back to the doorknob and, ignoring the searing heat, turned it and pushed the door open.

Lea peered into a small room. The light inside was

blindingly bright. Someone was in the room. But Lea couldn't see who. It was too bright. She had to shield her eyes.

Someone stepped forward, out of the light, a dark, faceless figure.

"Who are you?" Lea cried.

Without looking, she knew it was someone—or something—horrifying. Something hideous. Some creature bringing evil that was waiting to be unleashed.

"Who are you?" she repeated, raising her hands up as if to shield herself.

And the bright light faded. And the dark figure moved closer, came into focus.

"No!" Lea shrieked as she recognized the smiling figure looming before her.

It was Marci. Marci Hendryx.

Lea woke up. She sat straight up in bed, shaken, uncertain, bathed in cold perspiration.

She couldn't decide whether to laugh or cry.

This, her third week at Shadyside High, turned out to be a long week, a lonely week. Her parents busied themselves with fixing up the house and had little time for her. Deena had a new boyfriend, a tall, blond, skinny basketball player named Luke Appleman, and was spending all her time with him.

Lea had tried being friendly with Deena's friend Jade. But Jade was very popular and very busy, involved in a million clubs and with a million kids, and didn't seem to have much time for Lea.

Lea tried not to think about how lonely she was. But that was just about as easy as not thinking about Don Jacobs.

She had seen Don a couple of times during the week. Both times he was with Marci. Both times he gave Lea shy, apologetic glances before quickly turning back to Marci. Marci, of course, deliberately cut Lea both times, looking sharply away, an unpleasant scowl on her face.

Saturday night found Lea home alone again, her mom and dad at another party. She and Deena had plans to go to the movies at the Division Street Mall. But Luke called Deena at the last minute with two tickets to a rock concert at the big auditorium in Waynesbridge, and Deena, apologizing again and again, begged Lea to understand and went off to the concert.

Lea watched TV for a while, clicking the remote control, watching ten seconds of this and ten seconds of that, not really paying attention to any of it. She thought of doing homework, but decided that would be just too pitiful. She thought of going to the movie at the mall by herself, but that would be too embarrassing, especially since a lot of kids from Shadyside High were bound to be there.

Maybe I'll go rent a movie, she decided, clicking off the TV and pacing back and forth over the threadbare living-room carpet her parents hadn't replaced yet. She decided against it. By that time on a Saturday night all the good films would be rented.

Eventually, at a little after nine, she went up to her

room, planning to lie in bed and start the new historical novel her mother had taken out of the Shadyside library.

"Just what I need. An escape back to another century," she told herself.

She had read only a few pages when the sounds began above her head.

Tap tap. Tap tap.

Thump thump scrape thump.

Trying to ignore them, she turned the page and kept reading.

But the sounds grew louder, more insistent, as if urging her to listen, forcing her to pay attention.

Again, she thought she heard a voice up there. Or voices. Talking quietly, languidly, as soft as a rush of wind.

But not the wind.

Definitely not the wind.

Lea put the book down and got to her feet, her eyes on the ceiling. The locked room, she realized, must be right above her room, right above her head.

Thump scrape thump.

The voices up there rose and then faded.

This is driving me crazy, Lea thought, her heart pounding.

She remembered her dream. So silly. Marci Hendryx trapped in the boarded-up room.

And the other dream, the dream with the blood pouring down the door, the dream that was so real.

She pinched her arm. Hard.

I'm awake. I'm not dreaming.

This is real life—not a dream.

And the sounds were still up there.

I'm going up, she decided.

As she pulled herself up the metal ladder and struggled to push the trapdoor away from the opening, she was surprised that she felt less frightened this time.

She felt only anger. And curiosity.

What was going on? Who—or what—was making the noise? And why? Just to drive her crazy?

Dad's probably right. It's probably just a roof shingle, she told herself, feeling around on the wall and turning on the yellow light.

Her own shadow jumped in front of her, startling her.

Don't panic.

Surveying the long, low attic, she carefully made her way over to the boarded-up door, walking slowly, deliberately, listening hard.

She stopped at the door and leaned forward. She held her breath.

Yes.

She could hear voices.

Too low to make out the words.

But someone was in there. A girl. It was a girl's voice.

Her dream came back to her.

I'm awake now, she thought. Awake. Awake.

Lea pressed her ear against the door. Then, picturing the flow of blood down the doorway, thought better of it and pulled her head back.

She could hear the voice, but she couldn't make out any of the words.

"Who's in there?" Lea cried, not recognizing her high-pitched voice. "Who's there?"

She waited for a reply.

The voice on the other side of the door stopped.

"I know you're in there. I heard you," Lea called, too excited to be afraid.

Silence.

Even the wind outside seemed to stop its steady rush.

I'm going to solve this mystery once and for all, Lea decided.

But how?

"Are you in there?" she shouted.

Silence.

She raised both fists and pounded on the door.

"Are you in there? Can you hear me?"

She listened.

Silence.

Her heart was racing. Her eyes went out of focus, then focused again. She felt out of control. But there was nothing she could do about it.

She had to know who was walking around in there, talking, making those sounds.

Lea grabbed one of the two-by-fours and tugged at it. The heavy board wobbled in her hands.

It's loose, she realized. I can pull it right off.

She steadied herself and prepared to pull.

An earsplitting roar—the roar of a bomb blast— made her drop the board. She stood paralyzed by the deafening noise—just as enormous, pointed iron spikes shot out at her through the door.

chapter
8

*L*ea fell back, and the pointed spikes missed their target. As she stared in horror, the spikes slid back into the door before completely disappearing.

But the roar continued, echoing deafeningly through the low attic. She examined herself, gasping for breath, her legs weak and trembling. "I'm okay," she said out loud.

"Is this really happening?" she asked herself. "Is it real this time?"

She turned and ran to the trapdoor, jumping onto the ladder, nearly falling, finally steadying herself by grabbing the top rung with both hands.

Her heart pounding, Lea pulled the trapdoor over the opening and slid down the ladder onto the hall floor. She stood there for a long time, leaning against the cold metal, her eyes squeezed tight, trying to catch her breath, trying to stop her knees from shaking.

The roar was still echoing in her ears, as if it had followed her down the ladder. She shook her head trying to rid herself of it, and became aware of another sound too.

A ringing sound. Very nearby.

It took her several rings to realize it was the phone.

Taking in a deep breath and letting it out to calm herself, to slow her racing heartbeat, she made her way into her bedroom and hurried to the night table to pick up the phone.

How long had it been ringing?

"Hello?" Her voice came out shrill and tiny, like a cartoon mouse.

"Hello, Lea?" A boy's voice. Very familiar, but she couldn't quite place it.

"Yes," she replied breathlessly. "Who is this?"

"This is Don. Don Jacobs." The voice sounded tinny, far away. Lea could hear a car honking in the background, traffic sounds.

She started to talk, but no voice came out. Got to calm down, she told herself. Calm. *Calm.* She cleared her throat and tried again. "Hi, Don."

"Listen, Lea—uh, would you like to come meet me? I'm at the mall on Division Street."

"Meet you?" If only she could clear the roar from her ears. Did he say he wanted her to meet him?

Calm. *Calm.*

"Yeah. Can you?" Don asked. "I really would like to make it up to you. You know, for breaking that date last Saturday and everything."

Don't do it, a voice told her.

But Lea had to get out of the house, away from the roar, away from the noises and the room in the attic.

"Sure. I'll meet you," she said gratefully.

Yes! I'm getting *out* of here! Away from this creepy old house!

Again she saw the spikes, felt the imagined pain of them shooting into her body. Just a few minutes before.

"Where are you?" she asked eagerly, reaching up to push her hair into place, to straighten her bangs.

"What? I'm at a pay phone. It's very noisy here," he said, over a honking car horn.

"Where shall I meet you?" she asked, shouting into her phone.

"How about at Pete's Pizza? Do you know where it is?"

"I'm not sure. But I'll find it."

"Great, Lea. Great. Hurry, okay? Maybe we can still catch a movie. It's not too late."

"Okay. Bye, Don. I'm on my way."

Lea hung up and started to her closet, then back to the phone, then to the closet, then she finally stopped in the middle of her room.

Is the room spinning, or am I? she wondered.

She slid down onto the edge of her bed, breathing hard, and closed her eyes. She felt queasy. The roaring in her ears continued, just loud enough to be unsettling.

I've got to get out of here, she thought.

I can't believe he called. What good timing!

She jumped up, feeling quivery all over, still unable to shake away the fear.

Somehow she managed to pull some clothes from the closet, a clean pair of tan corduroy slacks and a new yellow Benetton sweater. Somehow she managed to get dressed and find the car keys and pull on her down jacket and lock the front door and back the car down the drive, the little ten-year-old Honda Civic that had become mostly her car. And somehow she had driven through the dark, unfamiliar streets to the mall.

It began to rain as she pulled into the nearly vacant parking lot. Most stores closed at nine. Several rows were still filled at one end of the lot—most likely they were near the movie theater, she figured.

The windshield wipers scraped noisily, smearing the glass, making it even harder for Lea to see as the rain battered down, attacking the little car.

What am I doing here? Lea thought.

Going to meet Don, she answered.

The thought cheered her. The sound of the rain made the roaring in her head finally disappear. She pulled into a spot at the end of the first row, cut the engine and the headlights, the wipers sliding noisily into place. Then holding her jacket over her head as a rain hood, she ran across the puddled asphalt to the nearest entrance.

The glass door was locked. Keeping the coat above her head, Lea checked in both directions and saw the signs for the movie theater to her left. As she jogged in that direction, the wind blowing a spray of cold rain onto her face, her sneakers splashed into a deep puddle. She felt cold water soak into the cuffs of her corduroy pants.

I'm going to look great when I finally get there, she thought miserably.

The rain let up a bit. The double-doored entrance beside the sixplex theater was open, and Lea eagerly stepped inside. She lowered her jacket and shook herself like a dog after a swim, water splashing onto the bright, patterned carpet.

Pete's Pizza was directly across from the movie theater. Lea could see that it was crowded, mostly with young people. Laughter and loud voices drifted out into the mall, along with the tangy aroma of cheese and tomato sauce.

Straightening her hair with her hand, she half ran, half walked toward the restaurant, pulling off the down jacket and tugging her sweater down. As she stepped through the open entranceway, the voices grew louder.

As she walked past the cashier in front, she saw Don. He was sitting in a booth in the middle of the restaurant, facing her. She gave him a quick wave, but he didn't seem to notice her.

"Hi, Don," Lea called happily, stepping up to the booth and starting to toss her jacket down.

And then she saw that someone was sitting across the table from him.

Marci!

"Oh," Lea uttered weakly, her mouth dropping open.

Marci turned to Lea. "What are you doing here?" she demanded nastily.

"I . . ." Lea looked at Don. But he only blushed and gave a quick, almost imperceptible shrug before turning away in embarrassment.

"I just wanted to say h-hi," Lea stammered, feeling her face redden.

Don was signaling her with his eyes now, obviously trying to tell Lea that this wasn't his idea, that Marci had just shown up.

"It's great to see you," Marci said sarcastically. "But Don and I really would like to be alone." She reached across the table and put her hand over Don's.

Don seemed to be very uncomfortable, but he didn't pull his hand away. "Uh—Lea, why don't you join us?" he asked.

He's really weak, Lea decided.

"No, thanks. I've got to go. Have a nice night," Lea said, trying to sound cool and together. But her voice quavered when she said it, revealing how upset she was.

She ran blindly toward the doorway—and collided with a waitress carrying a tray of sodas. The waitress screamed. The tray hit the floor with a clattering crash. Glasses shattered. A river of brown soda rolled over the floor.

"Oh—I'm sorry!" Lea cried, much louder than she had intended.

Everyone turned to gawk. Lea saw Marci and Don staring at her. Marci, craning her neck to see, had a broad grin on her face.

Ready to burst with rage, Lea fled into the nearly empty mall and kept running, her jacket held out in front of her, until she was back in the rain.

I could kill Marci, she thought. *Kill* her!

How could Don *do* this to me?

The steady rain felt cold on her hair, on her shoulders as it soaked through her sweater. But she didn't put on the jacket.

She walked slowly now, as if in a daze, not even sure if she was heading in the right direction. The rush of the rain drowned out all other sounds.

But she could still hear Marci's haughty voice repeating in her ears: "Don and I really would like to be alone."

I've never been so humiliated, Lea thought, rivulets of cold rainwater dripping down her forehead and cheeks.

Still carrying her jacket in both hands, she didn't bother to brush the rain away.

What did I ever do to her, anyway?

And what is Don's problem?

Is he totally terrified of her? Did he deliberately trick me? Did she make him call me tonight? Was it his idea?

He acted so embarrassed, so uncomfortable when I arrived. It *couldn't* have been his idea, Lea decided. Marci must have arrived *after* he called me.

Why did he just sit there? Why didn't he do anything to help me?

She opened the car door and tossed her jacket across the seat. Then she slid behind the wheel, totally drenched, shivering from the cold, but too angry, too *furious* to notice.

Never again, she thought, fumbling in her jacket pocket for the car keys. Never again.

Back to the dreary, empty house.

Up to her bedroom, pulling the wet sweater off over her head.

She took a hot shower and shampooed her hair, but it didn't make her feel any better.

I never would've gone if I hadn't been so terrified to stay home alone, she thought.

I never would've agreed to meet him if I'd been thinking clearly.

Well, now Marci will have another hilarious story to tell her friends, Lea thought bitterly, climbing into bed. And everyone at Shadyside will have another big laugh at my expense.

She could feel tears welling up in her eyes and fought back the urge to cry.

I could kill Marci. I really could.

Her bitter thoughts were interrupted just then by sounds above her head.

Footsteps again.

The ceiling creaked under their weight.

They were footsteps. No doubt about it.

Right over her head.

Thud thud thud.

Then back the other way.

Thud thud thud.

72

chapter

9

I won't be stopped this time, Lea told herself. I'm going to find out who is walking up there—and I won't be frightened away.

She had pulled on her robe and rubber thongs and was climbing the ladder outside her room. A fat, black fly buzzed slowly around the light fixture in the hallway, one of the last flies of autumn.

"Don't you know you're supposed to be dead?" Lea called to it, just to hear her voice.

She pushed the trapdoor up and away and blinked, surprised to find the attic light on.

Then she remembered that she must have left it on when she fled the attic earlier.

I'm not going to run this time, she thought, pulling herself up into the yellow light of the attic and climbing to her feet, wrapping the robe around her, retying the cloth belt more securely.

"This time I'm going to learn your secret," she said

loudly to the locked door. Talking out loud seemed to give her courage, to strengthen her resolve.

She stood a few feet from the door, studying it, her eyes moving slowly from the top to the floor.

No traces of blood. No iron spikes.

No roar.

She took a tentative step closer, the floorboard squeaking in protest beneath her. She leaned forward to examine the door in the strange yellow light.

The boards crisscrossing the door were covered with a thick layer of dust, she saw. They were lined with deep ruts and cracks, and were warped from age and from the dryness of the attic.

The nail heads protruding from the two-by-fours were rusted. One of the boards was nearly cracked in half and sagged in the middle, held up by only a few nails.

It was obvious even to Lea, who didn't have much knowledge or skill in carpentry, that the nails had been hastily pounded in. Many of them were crooked, the nail heads sticking out at odd angles. Some of the nails had been pounded in only halfway.

Whoever put up these boards, Lea thought, wasn't much of a carpenter or was in a terribly big hurry.

Mrs. Thomas, the real estate agent, had said that the door had been locked and boarded up for over a hundred years. The boards looked that old, Lea decided, but the door itself could have been put up the day before.

The wood was smooth and unblemished. It didn't appear the least bit warped or cracked. Nor did the brass doorknob show any age. It was bright, shiny almost, as if it were regularly polished.

Studying the door carefully, scientifically, made Lea feel more confident. She stepped right up to the door and, pressing her ear against the smooth wood, listened.

She pulled away quickly.

It sounded as if someone was crying on the other side.

Leaning both arms against the door, pressing her face forward, she listened again.

Yes. It sounded like a young person in there. And that person was sobbing.

"Hello!" Lea called excitedly. "Is someone in there? Can you hear me?"

She listened.

The crying stopped. There was only silence.

Then a girl's voice, muffled by the thick door, but clear enough to hear, called out to Lea. "Open the door! Please—open the door!"

Lea leapt back in surprise.

"Oh!"

There really was someone on the other side, someone locked in, boarded up.

But how could that be?

Taking a deep breath, Lea moved back to the door. "Who are you?" she shouted loudly.

Silence.

"Who are you? How did you get in there?" Lea asked.

Silence.

Then the girl's voice pleading again, sounding very frightened, very unhappy. "Open the door. Please—open the door."

Lea stared openmouthed.

Should she do it?

Should she open the door?

chapter

10

"*P*lease open the door!"

The girl on the other side of the door repeated her desperate plea.

"*Please!*"

Lea was frozen by indecision. A frightening picture flashed into her mind. She saw a hideous monster with red eyes bulging out of its sockets and green slime drooling from its fang-filled mouth. The monster was hulking on the other side of the locked door, disguising its voice, using the voice of a frightened girl in order to fool Lea. Once the door was opened, it would growl in its natural, disgusting, horrifying voice—and pounce.

Lea closed her eyes tightly and forced the gruesome picture from her mind.

"Please open the door!" the muffled voice, now even more frightened and desperate, called out to Lea.

"I-I'll be right back," Lea replied.

She had made her decision. She had decided to unlock the door.

Down the ladder. Through the hallway and down the stairs, her heart pounding, her mind racing crazily from thought to thought, wild pictures forming in her head of what the girl inside the room looked like. She found her father's big metal tool chest in the back pantry behind the kitchen. She shuffled through it, her hands moving rapidly, randomly tossing things aside, until she found the biggest claw hammer she could find. She found a small sledgehammer behind the chest and grabbed it too.

And then back up the stairs, tools in hand. She glanced at the clock on the kitchen stove as she passed. Nearly midnight. Her parents should be home soon.

What a surprise for them, she thought.

What a surprise for *everyone*.

Cradling the heavy tools in her arms, Lea struggled back up the metal ladder and hurried to the locked attic door.

"Are you still there?" she called loudly, dropping the sledgehammer to the floor.

"Yes." The voice sounded so tiny now, so far away. "Will you be so kind as to open the door?"

"I-I'll try," Lea said uncertainly.

"Please open the door!"

"I'm going to try!" Lea repeated as loudly as she could. The girl sounded so distant, Lea wasn't sure she could hear her.

Lea reached up and pulled on the highest two-by-four. It gave slightly and pulled away from the doorframe.

Not bad, Lea thought, encouraged. This may not be as hard as I thought.

She changed the position of her hands on the board, gripped it tightly, and tugged. The board was dry and had weakened over the years. It cracked and squeaked as one end pulled completely off the frame, leaving the nails in place. Lea used the claw hammer on the other end and pried it off quickly, almost effortlessly. She let the board fall to the floor at her feet, then bent over and tugged it out of the way.

One down, two more to go, she thought, pleased with herself.

The old boards were practically rotten, she realized. She pulled the remaining two off as easily as the first—she didn't even need the hammer—and dragged them to the center of the floor.

"Are you okay in there?" Lea called in.

Silence.

"Can you hear me? Are you okay?"

"Please open the door," the voice called.

"I'm trying!" Lea shouted. "I've pulled off the boards. Now I just have to figure out how to unlock the door."

"Please hurry," the girl called.

Lea bent down to examine the doorknob and the lock beneath it. To her shock, she saw a brass key in the lock.

"There's a key," Lea announced excitedly to the girl on the other side. "I can unlock the door now!"

"Please—unlock it!" the voice pleaded.

Lea paused for a brief moment, her hand gripping the metal key. Once again she pictured a hulking monster, covered in hair and slime and blood, waiting eagerly on the other side, cleverly calling to her in its best imitation of a girl's voice.

But Lea hesitated for only a second. Then she turned the key. The lock clicked softly.

Lea turned the knob and pulled open the heavy door.

chapter
11

*L*ea found herself staring into a beautifully decorated, old-fashioned-looking girl's bedroom. The room was lit with candles, two on a tall, mahogany dresser flickering against the back wall and one inside a glass hurricane lamp, glowing brightly from a low table in the corner.

The walls were papered in dark maroon wallpaper that appeared to be textured, like felt. A large canopy bed, all pink and satiny, with a heavy, quilted pink bedspread, practically filled the room.

And sitting on the canopy bed, her hands folded in her lap, was a girl.

The girl appeared to be about Lea's age. She was beautiful in a very old-fashioned kind of way.

Her hair was a mass of golden ringlets, worn without a part, the tight yellow curls tumbling onto her forehead and down the sides of her perfect oval-shaped face. A black velvet hair ribbon was tied across the crown of her head.

She had white skin that looked as if it had never seen the sun, and tiny features, small blue eyes, a perfect, straight nose, a tiny mouth.

She was wearing a high-necked white blouse that seemed as if it would be stiff and uncomfortable. Ruffles ran down the front, and the sleeves were long and puffy at the shoulders. Her black wool skirt came down over her shoes. It looked heavy and cumbersome.

She's like a little Victorian doll, thought Lea, staring in from the doorway. She's even smaller than Deena, and more angelic looking.

The two girls stared at each other for a long time without speaking. The girl on the bed sat very erect, keeping her hands in her lap. Nothing moved except for the flickering shadows caused by the candlelight.

Finally Lea got over her shock well enough to break the silence. "Who are you?" she asked. She was still standing with one hand on the door.

"This is my house," the girl said. Her mouth widened into a smile. Her eyes sparkled in the candlelight.

"What?" Lea gripped the door tightly.

"This is my house. I live here," the girl repeated. Her voice was tiny and sounded like a small child's voice.

"But how did you get in here?" Lea insisted. "I mean, up here? In this room?"

"Do you like my room?" the girl asked eagerly. She

slid off the pink quilt and stood up. She moved her hand in a sweeping motion, showing off her room. Her hand, like a small, white dove, fluttered in the long candlelit shadows.

"Yes, it's very nice," Lea said uncertainly, fear beginning to creep up her spine. "But I don't really understand."

"I've been so terribly lonely," the girl said, tilting her head to one side, the golden ringlets falling with it. "So terribly lonely, for so many years."

She's a ghost, Lea realized, staring wide-eyed as the girl slowly began to move toward her, a strange smile on her lips.

A ghost.

But that's impossible—*isn't* it?

"I've been so very lonely," the girl said, stretching her arms out toward Lea as she walked toward her. Her expression was so needy, so—hungry.

The girl shimmered in the candlelight, her image fading in the shadows, then growing bright again when she moved into the light.

A ghost, Lea thought.

Coming toward me, her arms outstretched.

"No!"

Lea hadn't even realized that she had uttered the cry. She began backing up, backing toward the safety of the attic.

"Please don't go," the girl pleaded in her tiny voice.

"You're a ghost," Lea mumbled, taking another step back, gripped with fear, heavy fear that weighted her legs, that made every step a struggle.

"I'm so lonely," the girl said, forming her small lip into a child's pout. "Can I touch you? Can I touch your hair?"

"No!" Lea screamed again, her terror making her voice high and hoarse. "No—please!"

"I won't hurt you," the girl said, her arms still outstretched, her face glowing in the dim candlelight, her eyes sparkling like pale jewels.

"No!"

Lea slammed the door shut and, struggling to control her trembling hand, turned the key in the lock.

Then she stood staring at the smooth wood of the door, licking her lips, swallowing hard, her mouth dry, her throat choked with fear, trying to catch her breath.

I never should have pulled off the boards, she thought. I never should have opened that door.

"Please don't go away," the tiny voice called from the other side of the locked door. "I'm so lonely. I just want to touch your hair."

"This can't be real," Lea said aloud. She turned and ran to the ladder.

She was awakened the next morning by the wind rattling her twin bedroom windows. The noise startled her awake. She sat straight up in bed. The room felt cold. The morning sky outside the windows was gray and threatening.

Her covers were heaped at the foot of her bed, and Lea realized she must have kicked them off in the night.

While I was having that dream, she thought.

It *was* a dream—wasn't it?

Lea had no memory of leaving the attic after seeing the ghost. She didn't remember turning off the attic light, or climbing back down the metal ladder, replacing the trapdoor, returning to her room, or getting into bed.

It had to have been a dream, she told herself. A very vivid and frightening nightmare.

So real. So many details.

But a dream nevertheless.

At breakfast she decided not to trouble her parents with it. Her dad had already been to the lumber yard, which opened early on Sunday mornings for people like him, and he and her mother were heatedly discussing their project for the day—the renovation of the screened-in porch on the side of the house.

They're so wrapped up in their plans, they don't even know I'm here, Lea thought. She felt amused by their childlike enthusiasm, but also a little hurt, a little left out.

As Lea was finishing her pancakes, sopping up the last drop of dark syrup from her plate, the phone rang. It was Deena, asking if Lea'd like to go to the indoor tennis club Deena belonged to and hit a few balls.

Lea dressed quickly, pleased by the invitation. Watching the sky grow more threatening outside her bedroom windows, she pulled on a pair of gray sweatpants and a matching sweatshirt. Then she searched her dresser drawers for a more appropriate tennis outfit to change into at the club.

It'll feel good to get some exercise, she thought. And I'll be able to tell Deena about the weird dream I had last night.

Deena picked Lea up in her parents' station wagon. Driving through the gray streets, a light, wet snow beginning to fall, she talked about Luke, her new boyfriend, telling Lea about the concert he took her to the night before, not leaving out a single detail, as far as Lea could tell.

It was warm and bright inside the domed tennis club, and most of the courts were taken even though it was Sunday morning. As they began to volley, Lea could tell right away that Deena was the better player.

They volleyed for a while, then played a game. "I really need a new racket," Lea apologized after missing two of Deena's serves in a row.

It's funny how people stare at their rackets after missing a ball or messing up, Lea thought. As if the racket were at fault and not the arm that swung it.

Deena eased up on her serve, and the two girls continued their game. "You have a pretty good backhand," Deena said as they changed into their street clothes afterward.

"You went easy on me," Lea said, a little embarrassed.

"A little bit," Deena admitted. "But only a little bit."

Both girls laughed.

Outside, the snow had stopped, but the sky remained gray and threatening and the sidewalks were wet.

As they walked to Deena's car, Lea began to tell her about the dream, about pulling the boards off the door, about the old-fashioned bedroom, and the girl behind the door.

As she talked, her breath formed puffs of white vapor in front of her. Like ghosts, she thought. Ghosts floating up and vanishing.

"And then I woke up and remembered every detail of the dream," Lea said, fastening her seat belt as Deena pulled away from the curb. "I could even remember the smell of the little bedroom. It had a wood smell, sort of piney, but stale smelling, old."

"Weird," Deena said, her eyes straight ahead on the road.

"It was very frightening," Lea told her. "Partly because it all seemed so real. And partly because the girl was so—so needy, so desperate for me to stay."

Deena drove in silence for a while, slowing to turn onto Lea's street, Fear Street. "I've never moved," she said finally, glancing at Lea, then back to the street. "I've lived in the same house here in Shadyside my entire life. So I don't really know what it must be like. You know. To do what you just did. Move to a new town, a new house, a whole new world. It must be pretty scary." She paused thoughtfully, and then added, "Especially living on Fear Street."

"Yeah, it is, I guess," Lea admitted. "But I've moved before."

"When you moved before, did you have bad dreams then too?" Deena asked thoughtfully.

"No. Well, yeah. I don't know. I really don't remember," Lea said, watching the old houses on Fear Street slip by, gray and ominous looking under the darkening sky.

"After you've adjusted," Deena continued. "I mean, after you've gotten used to the new house and everything, the nightmares are bound to stop, don't you think?"

"Yeah, I guess," Lea said doubtfully.

"You just have so many anxieties, and they have to come out somehow," Deena said, pulling into Lea's drive.

"Yeah, you're probably right," Lea said, gripping her tennis racket tightly in her lap. "Well, thanks for the consultation, Doctor."

Deena laughed. "You can write me a check later."

Lea reached for the door handle, but Deena grabbed her arm. The smile had faded from her face. "You know, I should tell you something," she said seriously, keeping her hand on Lea's jacket sleeve.

"What?" Lea let go of the door handle.

"Well—I don't want to upset you even more or anything . . ." Deena said, staring out the windshield.

"Deena—what?" Lea asked impatiently.

"Well, you've made a real enemy of Marci Hendryx."

"Tell me something I *don't* know," Lea snapped bitterly. She grabbed the door handle again.

"No. Listen," Deena said with some urgency. "Marci is spreading all these stupid stories about you all over school. She's saying that you're throwing yourself at Don, and that he thinks you're just pathetic. And she told some kids that you did the same thing at your old school."

Lea sighed wearily. "She's so mean."

"Well, just stay away from her. And stay away from Don too. Marci will do *anything* to hold on to Don. You really don't want her as an enemy. I wouldn't tell you all this, but—"

"No. I'm glad you did," Lea replied. She squeezed Deena's hand and then opened the car door. "Really. Thanks," she said, sliding out of the car.

"Talk to you later," Deena called out to her.

Lea watched her back down the drive, then lifted her eyes to the sky, dark as evening, the air heavy with the promise of more snow.

The old house loomed over her like a shadowy giant. Lea's eyes moved up the weathered shingles to her twin bedroom windows. Was someone staring down at her from the window on the left?

No.

It was just the reflection of a tree.

Get a grip on yourself, Lea, she thought, shivering.

The house seemed to laugh at her foolishness, a high-pitched whine of a laugh. It took Lea a few seconds to realize that the sound came from her father's power saw.

She could see him working on the porch wall. She called to him, but the power saw started its whining again, drowning out her voice.

Frowning, she gave up and hurried into the house.

She spent the afternoon helping her father. He usually insisted on doing everything himself. But that day he actually let her measure and mark some boards. And while he took a break to have a cup of tea, he reluctantly agreed to allow her to hammer in some nails. He stood right over her shoulder, watching every swing of the hammer intently, until she finally had to stop and playfully shove him away.

It was the first fun Lea had had in their new house. But it ended after only a few hours, when her mother returned from shopping with six venetian blinds that she insisted be put up in the downstairs bedrooms immediately.

That evening her parents were relaxing from their day-long home improvement efforts, watching TV in the den, a PBS nature documentary about gorillas. "They show the same gorilla show every week," Lea complained.

"These are different gorillas," her father said, straight-faced.

Lea went up to her room to take another stab at the chapter in the government text she should have read days before. The heat had come on. The radiator against the wall made a pleasant, steamy sound.

It's so warm and toasty in here, I hope I don't fall asleep, Lea thought, adjusting her desk lamp over the textbook.

She read for a few minutes, then stretched, the heat of the room making her feel drowsy as she had predicted.

And then she heard the soft thud over her head.

She slammed the textbook shut.

I'm fully awake now, she thought.

Or am I?

For most of the day she had been able to force all thoughts of the attic out of her mind. But, standing up, pushing her desk chair back, Lea realized she had to return to the attic.

She had to know the truth. She had to know if it had all been a vivid, terrifying nightmare or not.

Out in the hall she could hear the low murmur of the TV from downstairs. It was cooler out here. She felt wide-awake now.

Taking a deep breath, she grabbed the sides of the ladder and began to climb.

The door will be locked and boarded up, just as it had been for a hundred years, she told herself. Just as it was when I dragged Deena up here last Saturday night.

Deena really must think I'm crazy.

Maybe I am. . . .

The door slid away easily. Lea grabbed the frame and hoisted herself up into the attic.

To her surprise, the light was on, casting its pale yellow light across the low, narrow space. It took Lea a moment to catch her balance. Then, ducking her head under the low ceiling, she turned toward the hidden room.

"Oh!"

The cry escaped her lips as she saw the two-by-fours in a pile on the attic floor.

Just as she had left them in the dream.

Which wasn't a dream.

She stepped forward, leaned down, and touched

one of the boards, just to make sure it was real, it was solid.

Yes.

Then, without thinking about it, she stepped up to the door and, with a trembling hand, turned the key in the lock and pushed the door open.

The room was just as she had remembered it.

chapter

12

Lea gripped the doorknob tightly. She suddenly felt light-headed, unsteady. Her knees started to tremble, as if they couldn't support her weight.

"Don't be afraid," the girl said. "I won't hurt you. Really, I won't." She stood in front of the dresser at the back of the room, her hands at her sides, gently smoothing her long black skirt.

Lea stared wide-eyed at her, as if willing her to disappear.

The girl shimmered and seemed to fade for a second, flickered as the candlelight flickered.

I can see right through her, Lea thought, fascinated and horrified at the same time.

"My name is Catherine," the girl said, lowering her eyes shyly.

Lea exhaled noisily. She suddenly realized that she

had forgotten to breathe. Catherine watched her expectantly, waiting for her to reply.

But Lea was too frightened to tell Catherine her name, too overwhelmed to stand there and have a polite conversation.

She wanted Catherine to be a dream.

She wanted the room to be locked again, for the boards to be back in place. She wanted to be downstairs, safe in her room.

"Please—" Catherine started in her breathy, little-girl voice.

"Are you a ghost?" Lea blurted out, still standing in the frame of the doorway, her hand on the doorknob.

"Yes," Catherine replied without hesitating. Then she added with some sadness, "It took me so long to find it out. So many years to accept it. But, yes, I accept it now. I really have no choice, do I?" She raised her small white hands in a gesture of helplessness.

"And now you're going to haunt me?" Lea demanded.

In the shadowy light it was hard to tell if Catherine's expression was one of confusion or hurt. Her entire form darkened until she was just an outline, a billowing puff of smoke. Then, slowly, her face and body filled in again. She studied Lea for a while, then said, "I'm sorry. I do not understand."

"How did you get here? What are you doing here?" Lea asked.

"I told you. This is my house."

"But it isn't," Lea told her impatiently. "It's not your house. It's my house."

"Please come in and sit down," Catherine insisted, motioning to the edge of the canopy bed. "I won't harm you. I promise. I have been so lonely for so many years. I just want to talk."

Lea reluctantly let go of the doorknob and took a few steps into the room, making sure to leave the door fully open.

If she makes any move at all, I'll be out of here in a flash, she told herself. But she had to admit that Catherine seemed pretty harmless. And truly sad and lonely.

She looks like a sad little girl playing dress-up in those big, old-fashioned clothes, Lea thought.

"How long have you been a ghost?" Lea asked, standing in the center of the room, her arms crossed, as if for protection.

"I don't really know," Catherine replied, turning to stare down at the candle on the dresser. "I've lost all track of time. I've had no contact with the outside world. For a long time I just seemed to float. I wasn't in this room, and I wasn't anywhere. I was just floating."

As she talked her hair, a waterfall of ringlets, brightened to a golden glow, framing her perfect features in light. Her expression rigid with sadness, Catherine floated to a stiff-backed, wooden chair beside the canopy bed and sat down.

"At first I thought it was all a dream, a long, strange dream," Catherine continued. "But in time I came to realize the truth. That I was dead. That I had died in my own house. That I was now a spirit, a ghost. Merely a ghost."

She raised her pale, white hands and covered her face. Lea couldn't tell if she was crying or not, but her whole body trembled, faded into a smoky gray vapor disappeared for a brief second. When she reappeared a few seconds later, Catherine's face was calm, composed.

"You died in this house?" Lea asked. The girl seemed so small, so sad, so helpless that Lea found herself losing some of her fear. She sat down gingerly on the edge of the bed, sinking into the soft pink quilt and leaned toward Catherine to listen to her story.

"I was murdered in this house."

Catherine's words came out in her soft voice, flat and without emotion. Her chin trembled slightly, the only sign of the feelings behind the words.

"Murdered?" Lea suddenly felt chilled, despite the warmth of the attic room. The fragrant aroma of burning candle wax became too sweet, and she felt as if it would choke her.

"They said I was evil," Catherine whispered, as if revealing a long-held secret. "All my life from the time I was born. I was their evil secret."

"But why?" Lea asked. "What did you do?"

"What did I do?" Catherine laughed, a high-pitched child's laugh. The laugh turned scornful, then died abruptly, and her face darkened. "I was born. That's what I did. I was born, and they weren't yet married."

"I see," Lea said quietly.

"And so I became their evil secret. They locked me up, in this very room. They kept me prisoner here my entire life. They were afraid that someone would find out about me, that their precious reputations would be ruined."

Catherine faded until nothing remained but the chalky, white outline of her face, floating over the white, high-collared blouse. When she returned to view, her eyes burned into Lea's.

"Can you imagine the horror of it?" she asked. "My entire life spent in this tiny room, between these four walls, under this low ceiling. This room was my prison. My cage. And all because of something I had no control over—my birth.

"They were the evil ones. Not me," she continued, more loudly, her voice filling with vehemence. "They were the evil ones, so evil they would bring up a child as a caged animal."

She stopped for a moment and sighed, her sad eyes liquid, wet in the dark light, her hands clasped in her lap, hidden in the folds of the black skirt.

"I tried to escape," she continued after a moment. "I packed up my few belongings. I had been working on the door lock for months. I had it all planned. I didn't know what was on the other side of the door. I had never seen the outside world. But I could hear voices outside. The sounds of hoofbeats, of carriage wheels. I heard my parents and their friends downstairs. I knew there was more to the world than my tiny room. I knew I had to escape."

"And did you?" Lea asked, leaning forward, supporting her chin in her hands, drawn into the tragic story.

"My parents caught me as I was about to leave the

house. I fought them. They killed me." Her voice became flat again, flat and emotionless. The glow left her eyes. Her entire form darkened. "They killed me and brought me back up to this room, my prison, my cage. And then the cage became my tomb."

Lea looked away, turned her eyes to the flickering candles on the dresser top. She couldn't bear to see the grief, the look of betrayal on Catherine's face.

Neither girl said anything for a while. Then Catherine broke the silence. "I came to accept it in time," she said softly. "I came to accept the fact that I was no longer alive, no longer flesh and blood. That I was floating, floating through the years, a spirit reflection of myself. Look. I can make myself fade and disappear."

Catherine darkened to smoke, and then the smoke fell away.

"And I can make myself appear and glow more brightly than any living creature." The voice came out of air, but as she spoke, Catherine reappeared, the image brighter and brighter until her golden hair seemed as fiery as the sun, and Lea had to shield her eyes.

Catherine laughed, a bitter laugh. "There is only one thing I have not been able to do. I have not been able to leave this room."

Lea abruptly jumped to her feet. "No," she said, speaking more to herself than to Catherine. "No. I'm sorry. I don't believe this. I don't believe any of this. This isn't happening."

Catherine was on her feet too. Lea was surprised to see that she was at least a foot taller than Catherine.

'You *must* believe me," the ghost insisted. "You must!"

"No. I'm sorry. I have to go," Lea said, feeling the fear rise up from her stomach, choke her throat. "I'm sorry. This can't be real." She turned toward the open door.

"Please!" Catherine cried.

I have to get out of here, out of this horrifying dream, Lea thought. She started for the door.

"Please—I've been so lonely," Catherine pleaded breathlessly. "Just let me touch you. Let me touch your hair."

As Lea moved to the door, she felt her hair being grabbed. Cold fingers pulled at her hair, small, cold fingers, but strong, frighteningly strong.

"What beautiful hair!" Catherine exclaimed, tightening her grip, pulling Lea back by the hair and turning her around until they were face to face. Catherine's eyes glowed like black oil in moonlight. "What beautiful hair."

"Let go of me!" Lea cried. "Let go! You're *hurting* me!"

Catherine smiled and pulled harder. "What beautiful hair. We're going to be great friends—aren't we!"

"Let go of my hair!" Lea cried. "Please—let go of my hair!"

chapter

13

"*L*et go of me!"

With a scream of terror, Lea finally yanked herself out of Catherine's tight grasp and ran blindly from the room.

Into the harsh yellow light of the attic, a blur of shadows chasing her. Gasping for breath, her head still tingling, still aching from the cold fingers that had pulled her hair so painfully hard, Lea staggered to the ladder.

She dropped to her knees on the attic floor, flung herself onto the ladder, and, breathing hard, slid down to the hall floor.

"Oh!" She realized she had forgotten to replace the trapdoor.

Back up the ladder, her knees trembling, her whole body gripped with fear, she pulled the door back into place, then slid down again and hurried into her room.

She slammed the bedroom door and leaned back against it, closing her eyes, waiting for her breathing to return to normal, waiting for the aching in her head to stop, waiting for the fear to subside.

I'm okay, I'm okay, I'm okay.

She repeated the words again and again in her mind until they had no meaning.

Still shaking all over, she ran across the room and threw herself facedown on the bed.

I'm okay, I'm okay, I'm okay.

She buried her face in the soft bedspread.

And then pulled her head up sharply and uttered a low cry.

Did I close the door to the hidden room? she asked herself. Did I lock the door?

Or—did I allow the ghost to escape?

Would she escape? Would she come after me? Follow me down here?

Lea had the sudden feeling she was being watched. She pulled herself up to her knees, frantically surveying the room.

No. No sign of Catherine. No dark, ghostly vapors. No glowing blond hair. No pale, chalky face staring back at her.

But the door, the attic door.

It *has* to be locked, Lea thought.

I couldn't have left it open—could I?

Climbing to her feet, she knew she had no choice. She had to go back up to the attic and make sure the door was locked.

Lea knew she couldn't sleep, couldn't stay in her room, couldn't stay in the house if she had left the door unlocked—if Catherine was free—if the ghost was free to haunt her.

She took a deep breath and let it out. Catching a glimpse of herself in the oval mirror above her dresser, she stopped. She straightened her hair, pushing it into place with trembling hands.

Then she opened her door and stepped out into the hallway. Downstairs, the TV was still on, the murmur of voices and music floating up the stairwell. Lea hesitated at the foot of the ladder. She felt tempted to run down to the den and tell her parents what she'd done, and what she'd found in the attic. To tell them *everything*.

But, no, she first had to make sure the door up there was locked. She had to make sure they were all safe.

She pulled herself up the ladder. Her legs felt as if they each weighed a thousand pounds, but she forced herself to the top. She reached up and slid away the wooden door in the ceiling, then pulled herself up.

The light. The yellow light. She could never remember to turn it off.

Pulling herself to her feet, she turned toward the hidden room, holding her breath, dreading what she knew she was going to find.

But to her relief, the door was closed.

Closed—but was it locked?

She hurried over to the room, stumbling over the two-by-fours on the floor.

If only I had never touched them, she thought, with true regret. If only I had never pulled off the boards or unlocked the door or . . .

The key was in place. The door was locked.

Lea hesitated, listening.

Silence.

Feeling a little relieved, she hurried away. This time she did remember to turn off the light. The attic seemed to disappear completely in the blackness.

Yes. Disappear, Lea thought. Just disappear.

She lowered herself onto the ladder and pulled the ceiling door in place.

Safe in her room, she shut her door tightly.

Trying to calm down, she paced back and forth for a while, the old floorboards creaking noisily beneath her feet. Finally she began to feel more normal.

She reached onto the bed, picked up Georgie, her stuffed tiger, and hugged him close to her. "I'm afraid, Georgie," she whispered to the tiger. "I'm really afraid."

Lea stared as the tiger's eyes began to glow—red, redder, redder—until his entire face glowed with red, demonic evil.

Dropping the stuffed tiger onto the floor, Lea began to scream.

chapter

14

"Well, I couldn't believe it when she called Don," Marci was saying, pushing back her short, coppery hair as she talked. "But when she asked him out, it was just too much."

The crowd of girls around Marci burst into scornful laughter.

"And I was there at Don's house on the extension the whole time! I heard the whole conversation!" Marci exclaimed, delivering the punch line to her story, then grinning broadly, her pale blue eyes lighting up with delight, as the story received the laughter and approval of her friends.

Lea was standing right around the corner, hidden by her open locker door, listening the whole time, trembling with anger and embarrassment.

Marci really is sick, Lea thought. Marci couldn't wait to start telling stories about me to her friends. And such vicious lies!

Why is she doing this to me? Lea wondered. She's already won. She has Don. He's her total slave. He'll do anything she asks. When he sees her, he goes running, wagging his tail like an eager puppy.

And she's totally humiliated me. She's embarrassed me in front of Don, and in front of her friends. She's got the whole school laughing at me.

She's won. So why does she keep on doing this? It's sick. It's just sick, Lea decided.

She slammed her locker door and spun the combination lock. Adjusting the backpack on her shoulders, she turned the corner and headed down the hall to the front exit.

Two girls, pulling on down jackets at their lockers, snickered out loud as Lea walked by. Lea could feel her face growing red.

Friends of Marci, she thought bitterly, turning her face to the wall to avoid them. Angrily she jammed her hands into her jeans pockets and kept walking.

This isn't fair. Marci is ruining my life. *Ruining* it. And I haven't done *anything* to her!

"If only there was some way to get back at her!" she said to herself, pushing open the front door to the school and stepping out into a bright but blustery day. "Then maybe she'd leave me alone."

All the way home, first on the bus, then walking against the gusting wind, watching the swirl of leaves around her, breathing the sweet-sour autumn air, Lea dreamed up suitable revenges. But none of them seemed suitable enough.

I don't want to play any kind of dumb practical

joke, Lea decided. I want Marci to feel really bad, really grossed out, maybe. Really humiliated.

No. Really *frightened*.

Yes, Lea wanted to scare Marci.

A smile spread across Lea's face as she turned onto Fear Street, a funnel-shaped cloud of brown leaves swirling high over the street ahead of her, past the cemetery that sloped up to the right, the crooked old gravestones standing as silent, gray sentries.

Yes, I want Marci to be terrified, Lea thought, so engrossed in her schemes that she didn't see the squirrels that scampered just in front of her, on their way to scavenge for acorns in the old cemetery.

I want her to be as terrified as I was up in the attic last night.

Last night.

Yes.

The idea seemed to fall into place, so that by the time Lea unlocked the back door and stepped through the pantry into the kitchen, carefully wiping the wet soles of her sneakers on the mat by the door, she knew what she wanted to do.

The idea frightened her, but only a little. It would frighten Marci a whole lot more, Lea decided.

She tossed her backpack onto the kitchen counter, then checked the refrigerator door for messages. None.

Odd, Lea thought. Her mother almost always had some "emergency" instructions or news bulletins for her.

Heading to the front hall, she pulled off her coat and tossed it over the banister. Then she ran up the creaking stairs, cheered by her scheme, her eagerness to get back at Marci forcing away the fear she knew she should be feeling.

She's ruining my life. *Ruining* it.

The words ran through her mind, again and again, as she paced back and forth in her bedroom, thinking about her plan, chilled by it, excited by it.

Stop thinking about it and just *do* it, she urged herself finally.

Stepping out into the hallway, Lea pulled herself quickly up the ladder and slid back the trapdoor. She stepped into the attic, half expecting the boards to be back in place, the hidden room locked and boarded up, her encounter the night before all a vivid, mysterious dream.

But the boards were still on the floor. The smooth wooden door stood against the wall, exposed and inviting.

The fear returned.

Despite her excitement, despite all of her plans for revenge, the fear came back. Lea could feel her throat tighten, feel all of her muscles tighten as she made her way to the door.

A silent voice inside her, the voice of her conscience, most likely, her sensible voice, her realistic voice, told her to back away. Get out of there. Leave the door alone. Leave the ghost alone.

The voice told her to close up the attic. To stay away from there. To tell her parents about it. To tell her parents about Catherine. To let them deal with this. To let them face all the fear.

But that sensible voice was too quiet. It was

drowned out by a much shriller voice, a much more powerful voice, a much more compelling voice—the voice that called for revenge.

"Open the door!" Catherine called from inside the secret bedroom. "Please—open the door and come in."

Lea turned the key and, without hesitating to listen to her sensible voice, pushed open the door and stepped in.

chapter

15

"*I* didn't mean to hurt you last night," Catherine said nervously, her hands clasped at her waist.

She stood in the center of the room, dressed as before, in the high-collared, ruffled white blouse and the heavy black skirt that went down to the floor.

The same candles glowed on the small table and on the dresser. Lea suddenly realized that the candles in this room must burn but never melt.

"I didn't mean to hurt you," Catherine repeated, her expression serious and apologetic. "It's just that I hadn't touched anyone in so long. I—I forgot myself."

"That's okay," Lea said uncertainly. "I think I overreacted. I mean, I got scared and—"

"I won't do it again," Catherine interrupted

"My name is Lea," Lea told her, moving slowly into the room.

"It's a pretty name," Catherine said softly, shyly.

"You're very pretty. I like your hair. Such an interesting hairstyle."

"Bangs?" Lea exclaimed. "Interesting?"

"I always wanted dark hair," Catherine said, sitting down in the hard-backed wooden chair by the table.

"But your hair is beautiful," Lea insisted.

"Watch what I can do with it," Catherine said, a spark of playfulness lighting her eyes.

As Lea watched with a mixture of awe and fright, Catherine made her blond hair grow brighter, brighter, until the golden curls seemed to throb and flash, sending rays of light twirling around the room. Then, just as quickly, Catherine's hair darkened, faded until it was as dark as the black velvet hair ribbon she wore, and all of Catherine seemed to grow dark and shadowy until she was only an outline, a suggestion, a dim presence.

"Come back," Lea pleaded.

Catherine reappeared, obviously pleased with herself. "There are *some* advantages to being a ghost," she said, smiling. "There are things it is possible to do without a body. And then there are things . . ." Her voice trailed off.

"Would you like to come outside?" Lea asked, blurting out the words almost as a single word. She knew if she said them slowly, she would rethink them and not say them at all.

"What?" Catherine's pretty face filled with surprise.

"Would you like to leave the room? Come outside with me?" Lea asked, her heart pounding.

Catherine's smile transformed her face. She jumped

happily to her feet. "Yes!" she cried. "Oh, yes! Yes! Thank you, Lea! I don't know how to thank you! You *do* believe in me, don't you?"

"What?" It was Lea's turn to be thrown off-guard by a question. "Believe in you?"

"You do believe that I'm a ghost? And that I won't harm you?" Catherine asked eagerly.

"Yeah, I guess so." Lea didn't really want to think about that. In fact, she didn't want to think about anything. She wanted to *act*.

If she thought about it, she knew she'd turn back.

And it was too late to turn back.

"Where shall we go?" Catherine asked excitedly, clapping her hands together. "Where will you take me?"

"To a friend's house," Lea replied.

"A friend?"

"Well, she isn't really a friend. Actually she's an enemy, I guess you'd say."

Catherine's face filled with bewilderment.

"Her name is Marci," Lea said, deciding to tell Catherine everything before they began. "I want to play a joke on her, scare her a little."

"A little?" Catherine asked.

"A lot!" Lea corrected herself.

Both girls laughed.

"I'm beginning to understand," Catherine said, fussing with the tight collar of her blouse. "You want *me* to frighten Marci."

"Can you make things float?" Lea asked.

"I can make *myself* float," Catherine told her. "Is that what you mean?"

"No. I mean like, if you disappeared and lifted that candle holder," Lea said, pointing.

"Do you mean like this?" Catherine vanished from sight. A few seconds later the candlestick appeared to lift off the dresser top and glide through the air toward Lea.

"Yes! That's it!" Lea cried happily. "That's perfect!"

Catherine reappeared then with a soft *whoosh* of air, standing beside Lea, the candlestick in her hand. "This could be fun," she said, smiling. "I've never haunted anyone before."

"I want to convince Marci that I have evil powers," Lea said, unable to suppress an eager grin. "I worked out this whole idea on my way home from school. This girl has been so awful to me. I just want to pay her back so she'll leave me alone."

"I'll be happy to help," Catherine said, floating back across the room to replace the candlestick.

"You just have to follow my cues," Lea said excitedly. "Make it appear that I'm making all kinds of strange things happen. I want to terrify Marci out of her wits. I want to make her so frightened that she'll never dare to hurt me again."

"She'll never hurt you again," Catherine repeated quietly to herself. She took Lea's hand and squeezed it gently. Catherine's hand felt so cold in Lea's.

Cold as death, Lea thought. But she forced herself not to react. She didn't want to hurt Catherine's feelings.

"I cannot believe you are taking me outside,"

Catherine said, floating up joyfully off the floor. "When can we go?"

Lea glanced at her watch. "It's quarter to five. Marci is probably home right now. Let's go now, Catherine."

"Yes!" Catherine cried ecstatically. "Yes. Now. She'll never hurt you again. Yes!"

Catherine vanished from sight, startling Lea. She stared around the room, searching for her.

"Catherine? Where'd you go?"

Suddenly Lea began to feel strange. At first she felt dizzy. Then the dizziness became like a weight that pressed down on the top of her head.

"Catherine?"

Lea felt the weight press its way down on her head, down her shoulders and chest, then down on her entire body, lower, lower.

I feel as if I weigh a thousand pounds, she thought.

But then suddenly she felt as if the weight had been lifted and she became so light she might actually float away.

Then she had the sensation of losing control, losing all control.

"Catherine? What's happening?" Lea cried. "Oh— help! Catherine? Stop! Please stop! Catherine—what are you doing to me?"

chapter

16

"Relax, Lea," said a silent voice inside Lea's head. "I can feel the tension in your body."

"Catherine—where are you? What have you done to me?" Lea cried.

"It will be fine," the voice inside Lea's head said mysteriously.

"You—you're *inside* me!" Lea realized with horror. "Inside my brain!"

She was still standing in the attic room. At least, she *thought* she was standing. She couldn't feel her legs, she realized. Or her arms. Or anything.

Catherine has taken over my body, Lea thought. I'm still inside—but I'm no longer in control.

"It will be fine," Catherine repeated. This time the words came out of Lea's mouth—in Lea's voice!

"Catherine—please!" Lea pleaded. "I'm frightened. I feel so strange."

"I'm frightened too," Catherine replied in Lea's

voice. "I've never been outside before. I won't hurt you, Lea. I promise. And I'll separate myself from you when we reach Marci's house. It doesn't hurt, does it?"

"No," Lea admitted. "It just feels so strange. I feel so light, so weak. So out of control."

"I'm sorry if it frightens you. But it would be impossible to travel any other way," Catherine said, speaking softly through Lea's lips. "It would take all my energy. I'm not strong enough to travel any distance on my own."

"And you promise you'll get out of my body when we reach Marci's?" Lea asked warily.

"Of course," Catherine reassured her. "I am forever in your debt, Lea. You are so kind to invite me out. I don't want you to be frightened."

Catherine's words calmed Lea. In a few seconds she was descending the ladder, a passenger in her own body. A few seconds after that, she had pulled on her down jacket and was walking toward Marci's house.

"Marci lives on Hawthorne Drive, just a few blocks from here," Lea informed Catherine.

"It's so beautiful out here," Catherine said.

Lea's feet crunched over the carpet of brown leaves that covered the ground and sidewalk. The sun had already lowered, leaving only a few traces of pink and scarlet in a graying sky. The sweet and pungent aroma of burning wood filled Lea's nose. Someone down the block had a fire going.

"Everything is so magical, more beautiful than I ever imagined," Catherine said. Lea could feel warm tears sliding down her cheeks.

"I guess I usually take it all for granted," Lea admitted.

They turned onto Hawthorne. Marci's house was just a few houses down the tree-lined block. The houses here were rambling and old, in style not much different from the houses on Fear Street, only in better condition, the lawns carefully manicured and raked clean of leaves.

"It's so exciting to be in a real body again!" Catherine exclaimed. "To feel the air on my face. To feel the cold. Just to *feel!*"

"I'm glad," Lea replied with less enthusiasm than she had intended.

If Catherine likes being in my body so much, will she leave it when we get to Marci's? Lea wondered, her fear returning. Will she keep her promise?

What will I do if she refuses to leave?

"Here we are," Lea said as they walked up the gravel drive. Marci's house was white shingled, the shingles recently painted, with black shutters framing the windows, a sloping red roof on top.

As they stepped onto the front porch, Lea began to feel strange. For a brief moment she felt again as if she weighed a thousand pounds. And then she could feel the weight floating up, up, up from her body.

She raised her arm.

Lea was in control again.

She felt perfectly normal.

"Catherine?" she whispered.

"I'm right beside you," Catherine, invisible, whispered back. "I'm so excited, Lea. This is the happiest day of my life."

116

Catherine kept her promise, Lea thought with relief.
I guess I can really trust her.

She rang the doorbell. "Now let's see if we can *ruin*
Marci's day," she whispered.

Despite her excitement, Lea was suddenly filled
with doubt. What am I doing here? she thought. This
is crazy. Insane. I let my anger control me. I just
wasn't thinking clearly. This can't work.

But then she thought of Marci in the hall at school,
making up stories about her, and she remembered the
two girls who snickered as she passed. Her doubts
faded to the back of her mind.

Lea rang the bell again. She heard rapid footsteps
approaching from inside. The porch light went on
above her head. Then the door was pulled open
halfway, and Marci poked her head out, surprise on
her face.

"What are *you* doing here?" Marci asked coldly, her
breath smoking against the evening air.

"I—I want to talk to you," Lea stammered.

Marci's coldness, her obvious hatred, made Lea
want to shrivel up into a tiny ball and roll away.

"I'm kind of busy," Marci said, looking Lea up
and down, her face showing her obvious disapproval.

"Just a few minutes," Lea insisted, her anger returning, helping to restore her confidence. "I think we
should talk about a few things."

"Write me a letter," Marci snapped, and she pushed
the door hard to slam it.

But the door didn't slam. It remained open a few
inches.

Marci was pushing against it, but the door wouldn't close. She checked to see if Lea's foot was blocking it, but Lea was standing a foot back from the door.

"Hey! What's going on!" Marci cried, confused. "The door is stuck."

Catherine is doing a great job already, Lea thought, secretly pleased. She pushed past Marci and stepped into the front hall, ignoring Marci's hostile, suspicious stare.

"There's a reason I live on Fear Street," Lea said darkly, raising her eyes to Marci's. She had rehearsed that line all the way home from school.

"What do you mean?" Marci asked.

The front door slammed shut behind Marci. She jumped, startled by the noise. "What's with that stupid door?"

Lea laughed, nervous laughter she tried to disguise as evil.

"I want you to stop telling lies about me," she told Marci, staring into Marci's pale blue eyes.

"What? Why would I ever talk about *you?*" Marci asked scornfully. "Who are you anyway?"

"I heard you," Lea said, feeling surprisingly calm. "I don't know what you have against me, but I want you to stop."

"Have a nice night. You know the way out," Marci said, and started to move off.

As she passed the hall table with a tall, blue enamel flower vase on it, the vase suddenly floated up into the air.

"Hey—!" Marci cried. She stopped short, her back

against the wall, and raised both hands as if to shield herself from the flying vase.

"I *told* you," Lea said, enjoying Marci's being frightened, "there's a reason I live on Fear Street."

"What do you mean?" Marci cried, watching the blue vase descend back to its place on the table.

"I have powers," Lea said. "You picked the wrong person to have as an enemy, Marci."

"Now, listen—" Marci started.

But the coat closet behind her suddenly sprang open, and a khaki raincoat came dancing out, waving its arms, twirling rapidly.

"No!" Marci screamed. "Stop it!"

"I want *you* to stop," Lea said quietly, trying to keep a straight face.

Catherine is *great* at haunting people! she thought.

"This is all a stupid trick," Marci said uncertainly.

The raincoat collapsed lifelessly to the floor at Marci's feet.

"Get out of here, Lea. Go on. Get out," Marci insisted angrily, her back still against the wall, waving her finger at the front door.

"Oh!" Marci's mouth dropped open and she uttered a cry of terror as her feet suddenly left the floor and she floated up three or four inches.

Wow, thought Lea admiringly. For such a little girl, Catherine is really strong!

Marci kicked and struggled. "Let go!" she shrieked, her face bright red, her eyes round with terror. Twisting her body and thrusting her elbows back against her invisible captor, she broke free and fell heavily to the floor.

Panting, she scrambled to her feet. "Mom!" she screamed, pushing past Lea to get to the stairway. "Mom—help me!"

Uh-oh, thought Lea. Maybe Catherine went too far. Maybe picking Marci up was a bad idea.

"Marci—wait!" Lea called.

Marci was racing up the stairs, taking them two at a time, screaming hysterically, calling for her mother.

Lea watched from down below as Marci reached the second-floor landing, where a narrow balcony with a low railing stretched the length of the house. Doors opened off it. Marci started to run down the balcony.

"Mom!" she cried.

Marci's mother appeared from one of the bedrooms. "Marci, what on earth—!"

Marci was running toward her mother when suddenly, with a loud cry, she tripped and stumbled, grabbing at the wooden railing as she fell against it.

The railing gave way with a sickening *crack.*

As Marci's mother and Lea cried out in horror and disbelief, Marci plunged headfirst off the balcony, her hands frantically grabbing at air, grabbing at nothing —until, a second later, a second that must have seemed an eternity, she crashed to the floor below with a loud cracking sound, like that of an egg breaking.

chapter
17

"Oh, no! Oh, no! Oh, no!" Mrs. Hendryx was screaming over and over.

Lea reached Marci first. Marci was lying on her back, her eyes wide open, staring lifelessly at the ceiling. Her head was twisted at an odd angle. One leg was pulled up behind her back, bent the wrong way.

Lea, feeling for a pulse, leaned over Marci and listened for a heartbeat. Then she pressed her hand under Marci's nose to see if she was breathing.

"Mrs. Hendryx—I don't think she's breathing!" Lea shrieked.

"Oh, no! Oh, no! Oh, no!"

Still chanting her horror, Mrs. Hendryx dropped down beside Marci and cradled her daughter's head in her lap. "Call an ambulance! An ambulance!" she screamed.

Lea rushed to the phone and, her hands trembling, and pushed in 911.

"Oh, no! Oh, no! Oh, no!" Mrs. Hendryx was seated on the floor, rocking back and forth with Marci's head in her lap, Marci's leg still twisted behind her, bent the way no leg should bend. "She's gone. My baby is gone."

She was still rocking back and forth holding Marci when four paramedics and two young police officers arrived ten minutes later.

"It was a horrible accident, a horrible accident" was all Mrs. Hendryx was able to say before collapsing on the floor in tears.

The paramedics swung into action, pulling out equipment from their bags, working feverishly, trying to shock Marci back to life. But it was no use. She was dead.

"Marci and I were talking. Well, actually we had an argument," Lea told the police after the paramedics had called the family doctor for Marci's mother.

"Did you see her fall?" an officer asked, scribbling rapidly in his steno pad.

"Yes," Lea told him, choking back tears. "She ran up the stairs. She tripped, I guess. She fell against the railing and it—it broke. And she fell down here."

The two officers stared down at the body, but Lea couldn't face her. More uniformed men arrived. Marci's body was covered with a canvas tarp, and finally the coroner arrived.

There were more questions. More furious scribbling in steno pads. A doctor arrived to help Mrs. Hendryx. "A horrible accident," she whispered, her face blotchy and puffy from crying. She glanced at Lea as the doctor led her up to her room. "A horrible accident."

Was it an accident? Lea wondered, watching Marci's mother being helped up the stairs.

Was it an accident?

Or did Catherine murder Marci?

That wasn't possible—*was* it?

"Miss, I asked if you'd like us to drive you home," one of the officers asked impatiently.

"Oh. I'm sorry." Lost in her thoughts, Lea hadn't heard him. "Yes. Thank you."

"Follow me," he said, heading for the front door.

As she started to follow him, Lea felt the heavy sensation again. The weight pressed down from the top of her head and sank down through her chest and into her legs, until she was completely filled with the heaviness.

Catherine had reentered her body.

Catherine, I need to talk to you, Lea thought as she felt herself become almost weightless.

Catherine, did you murder Marci?

There was no reply to Lea's thought. Catherine was a presence, but silent.

Catherine, it was an accident, wasn't it?

I hated Marci, but I never wanted her to die.

Catherine, please tell me it was all a horrible accident.

Silence.

The nearly bare trees whirred by against the clear black sky. A few minutes later the two officers helped Lea out of the backseat of their black-and-white and accompanied her to her front door.

The porch light came on, and the door was pulled

open immediately. "Lea—what's wrong?" her father asked.

Lea rushed into his arms. "Oh, Daddy. Something terrible happened!" she cried. "A girl I know—she *died!* She *died!"*

Lea, overcome with the horror of the afternoon, could feel herself growing heavier again for just a second, and then the weight floated up through her body, through her head, until it disappeared.

Catherine had left her, most likely to return to the secret bedroom in the attic.

Mr. Carson, his arms around Lea, searched the officer's face.

"Your daughter is okay," one of them told him. "There was an accident. Her friend fell over a railing. It must have been a terrible shock for her."

Lea allowed her father to lead her into the warmth of the house. She heard the front door shut behind them. Then she could hear the cruiser roar off down the street.

"Lea—what on earth!" her mother exclaimed.

"It was an accident," Lea blurted out, unable to stop the tears that began to pour down her cheeks. "It was just a horrible accident!"

She tried to eat her dinner, but the cold chicken just wouldn't go down, and the mashed potatoes tasted like paste.

"I've never heard you mention this Marci," her mother said, sitting across from her, staring at her sympathetically.

"She's just an acquaintance. I mean *was*," Lea said.

"You've been through a terrible experience," her mother said, reaching across the table and taking Lea's hand. "You can eat later. Why don't you go up to your room and lie down for a while?"

"Thanks, Mom," Lea said appreciatively. She pushed her chair back and headed up the stairs.

But she didn't go into her room. She listened in the hallway to make sure her mom and dad weren't observing her. Then she silently climbed the ladder to the attic.

I *have* to know, Lea thought, pushing the ceiling door away. I have to know that it was an accident, that Catherine didn't murder Marci.

Because if she did murder Marci, then *I'm* responsible.

If she did murder Marci . . .

Lea didn't want to finish this thought.

It was freezing cold in the attic. Feeling very uncomfortable, she turned on the yellow attic light, then made her way to the secret room.

The door was closed.

Without announcing herself, Lea turned the key and opened the door.

Catherine was sitting on the bed, hands folded in her lap, as if she had been expecting Lea. A pleased smile crossed her face.

"Catherine—did you push Marci?" Lea asked without a greeting. A stern expression on her face, she stepped into the room and walked over to the bed, standing over Catherine.

Catherine's smile didn't fade. She looked up mischievously at Lea but didn't reply.

"Catherine—answer me," Lea demanded impatiently, hands on her hips. "Did you push her? Did you murder her?"

Catherine shook her head, her golden ringlets shaking with it. "It was a dreadful accident," she said, smiling up at Lea. "A tragic accident."

"I don't believe you," Lea said angrily. "You pushed her, didn't you!"

"You have no reason to say that," Catherine said in her teasing, little-girl voice. "You didn't see me."

"You were invisible, Catherine. I want to know the truth."

"I've told you the truth," Catherine insisted, looking past Lea to the half-open doorway.

"No, I don't think you have," Lea said. "I really think you floated up those stairs and pushed Marci."

Catherine rose to her feet and stepped away from Lea. She moved to the dresser against the back wall, then turned to Lea, her back against the dresser. "It worked out very well for you, didn't it, Lea dear?"

Catherine's tone, cold and hard, shocked Lea.

Catherine's face hardened to match her voice. She no longer was the petite young angel. Suddenly she was very old.

"Well? Admit it, Lea. It worked out very well for you. I helped you."

"You helped me?" Lea was staring hard at Catherine, astonished by the transformation.

"Yes, I helped you. And now it's time for *you* to help me," Catherine said, her face in shadow.

"Help you?" Lea took a step back. "Now, wait a minute, Catherine. I don't—"

Catherine floated away from the dresser, across the room, until she hovered over Lea. "Yes. You will help me now," she said, her voice hard, her eyes cold, her features frozen in contempt.

"No!" Lea shrieked and started to run. But the door slammed shut. Spinning around to face Catherine, she screamed at her, "What do you want?"

"What do I want?" Catherine tossed her head back and laughed, scornful, bitter laughter. "I want to be alive again."

"But, Catherine—"

"I want to touch things from inside a real body, Lea. I want to walk around, feel the ground, smell the air."

"But I can't do that for you!" Lea wailed.

"Of course you can," Catherine said, staring at Lea needily, hungrily. "You have to let me in now."

"What?" Lea didn't really believe what she was hearing.

"You have to let me in now," Catherine repeated, hovering over Lea. "I helped you this afternoon. Now you owe me."

"But, Catherine—"

Lea glanced over her shoulder at the door. It was shut tight. Catherine had done that. Maybe she had locked it too.

There was no point in trying to run.

But what *could* she do?

"You have to let me in," Catherine said softly, her voice pure menace, pure cold menace. "I'm coming in *to stay!*"

"No!" Lea pleaded. "Catherine—please!"

But Catherine had disappeared.

And then, Lea could feel the pressure on the top of her head, and she knew that Catherine was slipping inside her.

chapter

18

The first time Catherine had inhabited her, Lea hadn't known what was going on. She had felt the weight sinking through her body, had felt the new presence, and then had felt light again, light and out of control of her own body. But the experience had been so new, so terrifying, so completely bewildering that Lea could only stand passively and let it happen.

But now, as she felt her head grow heavy, felt the pressure begin to run down her back, she knew it was Catherine's invasion.

And she tried her best to resist.

"Get out! Get out! Out! Out!" she screamed.

And she concentrated with all her might, concentrated on keeping Catherine out, on keeping control of her own body.

"Out, out—get *out!*" she cried, her eyes shut tight.

Concentrate. Concentrate.

To Lea's surprise, it began to work.

She could feel the weight lifting, feel the pressure lighten.

Her head cleared. She kept her eyes closed, concentrating even harder, more resolutely.

"Let me in, Lea," Catherine, invisible, whispered from close by. "You owe me, Lea. Let me in."

"No!" Lea screamed and, opening her eyes, turned and ran to the door.

"Let me in, Lea. You can't resist me. I'm coming in."

But Lea turned the knob and pushed.

To her surprise, it opened easily.

She darted out into the attic, slammed the door, and turned the key in the lock.

I did it, she thought. I kept Catherine out. I forced her out.

Lea slid down the ladder to the second floor before she realized she was trembling all over, trembling so hard her teeth were chattering.

Calm down, calm down, calm down.

But she couldn't stop trembling.

"Mom!" she screamed, running frantically down the stairs. "Mom! Dad! Please! Help me!"

They came running out of the den, both of them with open mouths, their faces filled with fear and concern.

"You've got to help me!" Lea screamed, unable to stop the trembling.

Her mother ran across the dining room and wrapped Lea in her arms. "Lea—what?"

"It's a ghost," Lea murmured, pressing her face into the shoulder of her mother's soft sweater. "A ghost."

"Bring her into the den," Mr. Carson instructed his wife. "Lea, come lie down on the couch."

"No!" Lea pulled away from her mother. "I don't want to lie down! I *can't!* There's a ghost in the house. She murdered Marci, and I'm the one who let her out!"

"Lea—" her mother pleaded, her features pinched with worry.

"Lea, you're very upset," her father said softly. "You've been through a terrible ordeal. Now, just come into the den and—"

"No—I *won't* lie down!" Lea insisted, knowing she was out of control but unable to do anything about it.

"Then at least come sit down and talk to us," her father said patiently.

Lea sighed. "Okay." She followed them into the den and sat down on the edge of the brown leather couch.

Her father clicked off the TV. Her mother stood in the doorway, supporting herself with a hand on each side of the door frame.

"What's the matter?" Mr. Carson asked, sitting down beside Lea on the couch.

"There's a ghost upstairs," Lea began, trying to sound calm, trying to force her voice to remain normal. "A girl. In the attic. In the room behind the door."

"The locked-up room?" her mother asked, glancing at her husband.

"It isn't locked anymore," Lea confessed, looking down at the shaggy white throw rug at her feet. "I pulled off the boards, and I unlocked it."

"You did? When?" her father asked, sitting very close.

"Several nights ago. I thought I heard someone inside. So I pulled off the boards. I unlocked the room and found a ghost inside. A girl who was murdered in this house. A hundred years ago. And I let her out, and she deliberately pushed Marci over the railing. And now she—she wants—"

Lea's voice cracked. She stared at the rug. She couldn't continue.

"You've been through a terrible ordeal today," her father repeated. "I don't blame you for being upset. But we have to try to keep a sense of reality here."

"You don't believe me?" Lea cried, jumping to her feet.

Her parents were exchanging worried glances, signaling to each other.

"Lea, you're shaking all over," her mother said. "I'm going to find a doctor."

"No!" Lea cried. "I mean, I don't need a doctor. I'm not sick!"

"But, dear," Mrs. Carson said, "you're not making any sense."

"I'm sure you just need to rest, Lea," her father said, motioning for her to return to the couch. "I'm sure you just need some time to get over what you saw. It was an accident, after all."

"But that's what I'm trying to tell you!" Lea shrieked, pulling at the sides of her hair in frustration. "It wasn't an accident! Catherine murdered Marci!"

"Catherine?" her father asked, his forehead wrinkling in confusion.

"The ghost!" Lea screamed. "The ghost in the room in the attic."

"Lea, sit down," her father said firmly, standing up and pointing to the couch. "I really don't want to hear any more talk about a ghost."

"Let me try to find a doctor," Mrs. Carson said, biting her thumb the way she always did when she was nervous. She started to leave the den.

"Okay. I'll prove it to you," Lea said, still trembling. "I'll prove it to you." She grabbed her father's hand and pulled. "Come on. Both of you."

"You're taking us up to the attic?" her mother asked, following hesitantly.

"I'm going to show you the secret bedroom," Lea said. "I'm going to prove to you that I'm not crazy. That there's a ghost up there."

They climbed the stairs, passed Lea's room, and stopped at the foot of the metal ladder, all three of them lifting their eyes to the trapdoor in the ceiling.

"And if there is no ghost up there, will you let me call a doctor?" Mrs. Carson asked tentatively.

"There is a ghost," Lea insisted.

She climbed up the ladder as she had done so many times in the past two weeks, pushed away the wooden door, and lifted herself into the darkness of the attic.

Her parents followed. Mrs. Carson first and then her husband. "Ugh. It's so cold up here," Mrs. Carson complained.

It took Lea a few seconds to find the light switch on the wall. She pushed it and yellow light flooded the long, narrow room.

Breathing hard, Lea led the way to the hidden room.

And then stopped short with a loud, disbelieving gasp.

The door was closed and locked.

The boards were all in place, blockading the doorway, nailed sturdily over the door.

Nothing had been touched. It all looked the same as it had the day they moved in.

chapter

19

Dr. Harrison clicked his bag shut. He straightened Lea's blanket, then smiled down at her through his wire-rimmed bifocals. "You'll be okay," he said, his face expressionless, businesslike. "You've got quite a fever. But we'll bring it down. Stay in bed a few days, okay? At least till the fever is gone."

Feeling drowsy from the high temperature, Lea thanked the doctor. She turned her face into her pillow.

They don't believe me about Catherine, she told herself bitterly. They think the fever was giving me hallucinations.

Across the room rain drummed against the twin windows. A strong wind drove waves of water against the glass, making the old window frames rattle.

Lea could hear Dr. Harrison out in the hall, talking in hushed tones to her parents. She raised her head from the pillow and tried to make out what he was saying. But he was talking too quietly.

A few seconds later she heard the three of them go down the stairs. She heard the front door close as the doctor left.

They think I imagined it all, Lea thought.

Maybe I did. . . .

She looked up to see both of her parents enter the room, walking softly, almost tiptoeing. "Still awake?" her father whispered.

"I feel very sleepy," Lea said, yawning.

"Dr. Harrison says the fever has broken," her mother said, biting her thumb nervously as she leaned over Lea, studying her as if seeing her for the first time.

"Stop looking at me like that," Lea said, wondering why her voice was so hoarse.

"You just need to stay in bed for a few days. You know. Rest up," her father said.

"I feel like I could sleep for a week," Lea replied.

Her mother leaned down and kissed her forehead. She smelled of oranges. Lea smiled and closed her eyes.

A strong burst of rain against the windows made her open them again. Her parents had gone downstairs. She picked up Georgie from the foot of the bed and held him close. "They think I'm crazy, Georgie," she told the stuffed tiger.

As if in reply, Georgie's eyes began to glow bright red.

"No!" Lea whispered, and tossed the tiger to the floor.

When she looked up, Catherine was standing beside the bed, bathed in the same harsh red light that had come from Georgie.

"Catherine—what are you doing here?" Lea asked, feeling very groggy. "How did you get down here?"

"This is my room," Catherine replied, smiling down at Lea.

The red glow faded. All the color in the room seemed to fade until there were just two circles of red light, glowing red light coming from Catherine's eyes.

"Your room? What do you mean?" Lea pulled herself up to a sitting position, leaning her head against the hardwood headboard.

"This is my room," Catherine repeated, still smiling. "I've been in this room all along."

"But the room upstairs. The secret bedroom—" Lea started.

"*This* is the secret bedroom," Catherine told her, sitting down on the edge of the bed, her eyes still glowing. "This is my bedroom. You were never in the room upstairs, Lea."

"Never?" Lea's head spun. She closed her eyes.

I really *am* crazy, she thought.

Rain pounded against the window. Lea felt a wisp of cold air on her face, a draft from the window. She pulled the blanket up to her chin and gripped it tightly, as if it could protect her from Catherine, from what Catherine was telling her.

"You were never in the hidden room," Catherine explained in her soft, little-girl voice. "You were never in the room upstairs—because *I* was never in the room upstairs. I never left *this* room."

"I don't understand," Lea said, opening her eyes, staring back at the pale, ghostly girl.

"I invaded your mind, Lea," Catherine explained in a flat, emotionless tone. "I gave you visions. I made you believe you were upstairs in the secret bedroom. But that room has been boarded up all along. You were down here in your bedroom the whole time."

"But why? Why?" Lea asked. The blanket gripped tightly up to her chin wasn't keeping out the cold, the cold fear that had swept over her entire body.

"That room upstairs is evil," Catherine said. Her eyes glowed bright scarlet as she said this. She floated up off the bed, hovering over Lea, the light from her eyes burning Lea's face.

Lea turned her head away.

Catherine eased back onto the edge of the bed. "It's evil. I boarded the room up myself. A hundred years ago. I did it. And that door will stay locked *forever*."

Lea didn't say anything. She felt so sleepy. It was hard to concentrate on Catherine's words. It was hard to make sense of them.

"I saw you go up to the attic the first time," Catherine continued. "I saw you approach the boarded-up door. I saw you listening there. At first, I tried to scare you away from it."

"You mean—?" Lea remembered those first frightening visits to the attic.

"Yes. The dripping blood and the metal spikes. I did that," Catherine said. "I had to scare you. I had to keep you away from that room of evil. But it wasn't enough. When I saw you were determined to open the door, to enter the room, I invaded your mind. I made you think you were upstairs. I made you think you had opened the door. But you were down here in your bedroom the whole time."

Catherine laughed, a high-pitched giggle that made her golden ringlets tumble and shake. It was obvious that she was bragging, pleased with herself, with the trick she had played on Lea.

"But why did you go to all that trouble?" Lea asked in her husky voice. "Why did you make me think I was upstairs?"

"So you wouldn't be afraid to be in your own bedroom," Catherine replied, as if the answer were obvious. "I needed you to be comfortable. I needed you to feel sorry for me, to sympathize with my sad story. I needed you to believe in me."

Lea shifted uncomfortably, gripping the blanket even tighter with both hands, feeling cold, so cold she started to shiver. "What's going to happen now, Catherine?" she asked, her teeth chattering.

"Now we're going to share this room," Catherine said, leaning close. "And your body."

"No!" Lea tried to scream, but she felt too weak, too sleepy, too dizzy.

"Now you are mine!" she heard Catherine cry.

And then she could feel the weight on her head, feel the heavy pressure drop down through her body. Heavy. So heavy.

She knew Catherine was invading her, possessing her.

But Lea was too weak, too sleepy to resist.

In a few seconds Catherine had taken full possession. "How lovely!" she said cheerfully in Lea's voice.

chapter

20

Catherine had taken over.

During the next few days, as she waited around the house for her temperature to return to normal, Lea felt like a visitor in her own body. She was conscious. She was alert to everything that was going on. But she had no control over what she said or did.

She had no voice. She could only think.

She still had a will, but she could only follow.

It was Catherine's body now.

Lea would argue with Catherine, try to convince Catherine to leave her alone. But Catherine ignored Lea's silent pleas.

As if Lea didn't exist.

Sometimes, without warning, Lea would suddenly feel Catherine's presence float out from her body. These times filled Lea with hope and relief. Back in charge of her body, she felt like crying or leaping for joy.

But she was always too tired.

And too frightened.

And then, too short a while later, she would feel Catherine reenter, taking over once again. And Lea returned to her frightening position as a silent partner, a silent partner in her own body!

Where did Catherine go when she left Lea's body?

Lea never asked. Catherine would most likely ignore her question anyway.

Catherine was in charge now.

Catherine was the only one allowed to ask questions.

One morning, when Catherine had disappeared for a short while, Lea nearly told her mother what was happening. But she stopped herself just in time.

If I tell her I'm being possessed by a ghost, that a ghost is controlling my every word and act, I'll spend the rest of my life locked up in a hospital somewhere, Lea realized.

So she resisted the temptation, and soon afterward Catherine returned. "Maybe we can go out today," Catherine told her. "Maybe we are finally strong enough to leave the house. I have some big plans for us, Lea. Some very important things we must do."

Lea, dreading the answer, asked what Catherine had planned. But once again her silent question was ignored.

"You seem to be doing fine," Lea's mother said cheerily, bursting into the room, pulling back the curtains from the twin windows, revealing a clear, sunny day. "Why don't you take a walk or something today? Get out of this stuffy house."

"Yaay!" Catherine yelled in Lea's voice. She kicked off the covers and climbed to her feet.

"Now, don't overdo it," Mrs. Carson said, pulling open one of the windows to let some cold, fresh air into the room.

"I won't," Catherine told her. "It's such a pretty day. Maybe I'll just go for a short walk."

"Just promise you won't overdo it," Mrs. Carson said, looking concerned. "You've been a pretty sick young lady."

"I feel great!" Catherine said.

When Mrs. Carson went back downstairs, Lea pulled on a pair of black denims and a maroon and gray Shadyside High sweatshirt and then began searching the cluttered floor of Lea's closet.

"What are you doing?" Lea asked silently. "Catherine, what are you looking for?"

Catherine didn't reply as Lea's hands continued to search. Then, finally, mysteriously, she said, "Big plans, Lea. Big plans. Aha! Here it is."

She pulled a piece of heavy twine out of the closet, twine that had held together the last of Lea's cartons that had finally been unpacked.

"Catherine—what are you going to do with that?" Lea demanded.

"You mean, what are *we* going to do with it," Catherine said mischievously. *"We* are going to have a little fun." Lea had no control. Against her will, she felt herself pull the coarse twine taut, then snap it between her hands. "We're going to teach Don Jacobs a little lesson," Catherine told her.

"Huh?" Lea wasn't sure she had heard correctly. "Don?"

"He and Marci were real close, right?" Catherine asked. But it wasn't a question. "I heard everything, Lea. I heard you telling everything to Deena on the phone. I was in your bedroom all the time, remember?"

"But Don—" Lea started.

"Don needs to be taught a lesson too," Catherine said coldly. "Come on. Let's go, Lea. Let's see what you can do."

chapter
21

Don lived in a square, red-brick house on Canyon Road. Someone must have spent the entire morning raking leaves, Lea realized, for an enormous leaf pile stood in the middle of the small front yard.

"What a beautiful walk we've had," Catherine said silently to Lea. "The air—it smells so fresh and sweet. I think autumn is my favorite time of the year."

Lea responded with glum silence. She had argued with Catherine the entire way over to Don's house, trying to stop her from carrying out whatever horrid plans she had for Don.

"But I'm doing it for *you,* dear" was Catherine's only reply, and then she chose to ignore Lea entirely.

When they had reached Don's block, Lea made one last desperate effort to regain control of her body. She concentrated on driving Catherine away, on making her legs stop.

But Lea was too weak.

Catherine was firmly in charge.

Despite Lea's efforts, her legs kept moving, she continued walking briskly over the leaf-strewn sidewalks toward Canyon Drive and Don's house.

"It's no use trying to resist," Catherine told her as they walked up the asphalt drive. "I'm doing this for you. Don was such a little slave to Marci. He never stood up for you."

"Catherine, *please*—" Lea begged.

But she was ringing the doorbell.

Please don't be home, Lea thought. Please don't be home.

Footsteps inside. The white front door was pulled open. Don stood in the doorway, a startled look on his face. "Lea!"

"Hi, Don," Catherine said in Lea's voice. "How are you?"

"Lea—how are *you?*" Don asked, holding open the storm door. "I heard you were sick."

"I'm okay now." She stepped into the small entranceway. The house smelled of roasting chicken. She could hear heavy metal music blaring from somewhere upstairs.

"What a surprise," Don said, wiping his hands on his sweatshirt. "I just finished raking leaves. Some guys are coming over, and—"

"I'll only stay a minute," she said. "I wanted to see how you were doing. I mean, you must've been pretty broken up. About Marci."

Don lowered his head, averting his eyes. "Yeah," he muttered.

The room was silent for a moment, except for the music from upstairs.

"It was pretty tough," he said finally, still avoiding her glance. "Such a shock. I mean, such a stupid accident. It was—unbelievable."

"Yes. Unbelievable," she repeated softly.

Lea listened helplessly as the conversation continued, Catherine speaking so sympathetically to Don, poor, unsuspecting Don.

If only there was something I could do, Lea thought desperately. Some way to stop Catherine.

But Lea was helpless. A helpless bystander.

"You were there," Don said. "It must have been horrible for you."

They were still standing awkwardly in the entranceway. Don had his hands jammed into his jeans pockets.

"Yes, it was," she said softly, shaking her head. "I—I don't think I'll ever get over it."

"I feel really alone now," Don confessed, raising one hand to scratch the top of his curly brown hair.

"Well, you shouldn't feel alone," Lea said meaningfully.

Don stared back at her for a long moment. Then his mouth dropped open as he suddenly remembered something. "The chicken! My mom went out. I promised her I'd turn off the oven."

He turned and hurried to the kitchen.

As soon as he was out of sight, Lea reached into her jeans pocket and pulled out the length of twine. She held it between her hands, untangling it.

146

"Catherine—what are you going to do?" Lea demanded.

No reply.

Lea felt her body begin walking toward the kitchen.

"Catherine—stop. What are you going to do?"

No reply.

Walking silently, Lea crept into the kitchen. She stepped quickly behind Don, who had his back turned. He was bending over the open oven, checking the chicken.

She pulled the rope taut and began to raise it over Don's head.

With a silent gasp of horror Lea realized that she was about to strangle Don.

chapter
_____

22

Lea leaned forward until she was almost on Don's back, raising the twine over his head, ready to pull it around his neck and choke him with it.

The doorbell rang.

Don stood up straight.

Lea backed away quickly, letting go of the twine, letting it fall to the floor.

"Hey!" Don cried, spinning around. "I didn't hear you come in here."

"Sorry," Lea said.

That was a close one, Lea, helpless in her own body, thought, greatly relieved.

And then, shaken with fear, she realized that Catherine hadn't been defeated. Only delayed. She would try again.

And Lea would be a murderer. A true murderer.

Don turned off the oven and ran to the front door. Lea stopped to retrieve the twine, jamming it hurriedly into the pocket of her jeans, then followed Don to the front hall.

"Hi, guys," Don was saying. "I'm all ready. Just have to get my keys."

Two boys Lea recognized from school, Cory Brooks and Gary Brandt, strode into the house. They were both wearing jeans and Shadyside High letter jackets.

"Hey, you know Lea?" Don asked, heading into the living room. "Lea Carson, this is Cory and Gary," he called out.

"Hi," Lea said shyly.

"How ya doin'?" Cory asked.

"I've seen you at school," Gary said. "Are you in Hunter's chemistry class?"

"Yeah," Lea said. "I just started a few weeks ago."

"Okay. Let's go," Don said, reappearing. He had brushed his hair in the few seconds he'd been gone. "Can we give you a lift anywhere, Lea?"

"No. Thanks," Lea said. "I'm going to walk." She started out the front door. "See you soon, Don. Take care."

I don't *believe* this, Lea thought. First Catherine tries to strangle him. Then she tells him to take care.

"Nice meeting you guys," Lea called back to Gary and Cory, and then started to jog down the driveway, past their car, a beat-up Ford Fiesta with radio-station bumper stickers pasted all over the back, and down Canyon Road, jogging against the wind, cold and fragrant on her burning hot face.

"Did you have a nice a nice walk, dear?" Mrs. Carson asked, hearing Lea return.

"Very pleasant," Catherine replied in Lea's voice. "I'm beginning to feel so much better, Mom."

"Oh, I'm so glad," Mrs. Carson said, entering the room, wiping her hands on a dish towel.

"I'm really sorry," Lea said, "you know, about the ghost stuff, the crazy things I said. I must have really worried you, Mom."

Listening to this, helpless to interfere, Lea uttered a silent plea: It isn't me, Mom. It isn't me saying those words. Please, Mom. Can't you *tell?* Can't you tell that it isn't me?

"Your dad and I were a little worried. You were obviously having some sort of hallucinations from the high fever, Lea," Mrs. Carson said.

"Well, I feel really good now," Lea said cheerily. "Like my old self."

She started up the stairs to her room.

"Catherine, you can't *do* this to me!" Lea cried, a silent, desperate plea.

"He'll die next time," Catherine muttered in a dark, terrifying voice to Lea. "Don will die, and so will his stupid, grinning friends. They'll die too. They'll *all* die."

The blackness seemed to part, and behind it lay more blackness. Then two rectangles of gray came into focus. The two windows across the room.

Lea sat up as the swirling shades of black lifted and her room settled into place.

She felt strange, unsettled.

"Catherine?" she whispered.

No reply.

150

And then Lea realized. Catherine had left her body again.

"Catherine?"

Lea had no idea how long Catherine would be gone. Sometimes it was for a few hours, sometimes for only minutes.

Where does she go? Lea wondered.

She spun around in her silky, white pajamas and put her feet on the floor. I'm moving, she thought. I'm moving my legs, my body. I'm doing the thinking. I'm in control.

It felt so good, if only for a short while.

I've got to do something, Lea thought. I've got to get rid of Catherine.

Before she kills Don.

But how? What can I do?

She wrapped her arms tightly around herself, suddenly feeling very alone.

I have no one, she thought miserably. There's no one I can tell. No one I can turn to. If I tell my parents, they'll call the doctor, and I'll be in bed for the rest of my life. If I tell Deena—well, she wouldn't believe me, either.

No one would believe me.

I'm all alone, and I've got to deal with Catherine on my own.

But how?

And then she had an idea.

The locked room. The boarded-up room in the attic.

The secret must be up there, Lea decided.

Why else would Catherine be so desperate to keep

me away from it? Why would she pull all those tricks, give me visions to make me think that I was in that room, do everything she could to keep me out of it?

Lea remembered Catherine saying that she had boarded up the room herself, that she wanted it to stay boarded up forever.

Why?

There was something in that room that Catherine didn't want to let out. A secret. A secret frightening to Catherine.

I have to know what it is, Lea decided, climbing to her feet. I have to find out what's behind the locked attic door.

chapter
23

*T*he attic was still and cold, the air thick
and hard to breathe. Lea nearly choked on the sour,
stale dust that invaded her nostrils.

She clicked on the attic light and moved quickly,
her rubber thongs padding over the creaking floorboards, to the boarded-up door.

When will Catherine be back? she wondered, the
thought sending a chill down her back.

"Catherine?" she called.

No reply.

When will she be back?

I've got to hurry. I've got to learn the secret of this
room before Catherine returns, before she can stop
me, before she can invade my body again.

Without hesitating any longer, she grabbed the
highest two-by-four and tugged. It didn't budge. She
tugged again. It was securely nailed.

The boards came off so easily before, she recalled. But that, of course, was just a vision, just a dream.

A hammer. She needed a hammer.

But was there time?

Lea had no choice. Down the ladder, then down the stairs. She crept through the dark, silent house to the back, her eyes adjusting to the dim light, the familiar objects around her strange and mysterious in shades of black.

It took a while to find her father's tool chest, and a while longer to rummage through it in the dark, quietly, oh, so quietly, to find the claw-headed hammer.

Then back up to the attic.

Catherine? Where was she?

About to return? About to pounce? About to stop Lea before she could learn the hidden room's secret, the only secret that could possibly save her?

Back into the attic cold, the choking sourness of the dust.

And now she was pulling frantically at the boards, wedging the hammer between the doorframe and the board, pushing and prying with all her strength. Frantic motions, desperate motions. So frightened. Listening for any sound, watching for any clue that Catherine might be returning.

The first board groaned as if in protest and fell to the floor. She started on the second one, breathing hard, coughing on the thick, dusty air, listening, waiting, every pore on edge, every pore alert as she feverishly worked the hammer, prying loose that board too.

The second board fell with a soft thud, kicking up dust as it landed.

One board to go. And then she could pull open the door.

"Catherine?"

No reply.

Still not there. Maybe there was time. Maybe Lea could do it.

The third board resisted her efforts. She wedged the hammer in and pulled. It squeaked and groaned but didn't move. She was bathed in sweat now, cold, uncomfortable sweat. But she continued to work feverishly.

Until the third board came off and fell at her feet.

She was reaching to turn the key in the door lock when a voice cried out right beside her.

"Lea—what are you doing?"

Catherine was hovering beside Lea, her eyes glowing red with fury, her tiny features twisted in anger, her golden ringlets flying wildly about her head.

"What are you doing? Get *away* from that door!"

Lea ignored her and reached for the key.

But with astounding strength, Catherine grabbed Lea by the shoulders and pulled her back.

"No!" Lea screamed. "You can't stop me!" She ducked, pulled out of Catherine's cold grip, and stumbled forward to the door. Then she grabbed the key and started to turn it.

But Catherine moved quickly. She floated above Lea, then vanished.

And Lea felt the pressure on the top of her head, felt

Catherine begin her invasion, felt the weight begin to descend.

Leaning against the locked door, Lea jammed her eyes shut and concentrated.

I kept her out once, she thought. I shut her out once. I can do it again. I just have to be strong . . . strong . . . strong. . . .

But the pressure built until her head felt about to explode. Catherine was pushing her way in, determined to stop Lea, determined to take control once again.

No, no, no, no. Lea concentrated on keeping the ghost out.

The weight began to lift, the pressure lighten.

Yes!

She had done it.

"Don't open the door!" Catherine, invisible, shrieked from somewhere, somewhere *outside* of Lea. "Don't!"

I've shut her out, Lea thought, her heart pounding. I've shut her out.

"Lea—*don't!*"

Lea turned the key and pulled open the door.

She peered into the room, raised her open hands to her face—and started to scream.

chapter

24

The bedroom was revealed much as Lea
had imagined it—the dark walls, the flickering candles, the canopy bed.

But sitting on the bed were a man and a woman. Or,
as Lea observed now, the horrible *remains* of a man
and a woman.

They were dressed entirely in black, which made
them difficult to see in the shadowy light. The woman
wore a long, flowing, high-necked dress; he a dark suit
and white shirt with a stiff collar. The clothes appeared to be in good condition and clean, but hung in
folds on them, many sizes too big.

Staring into the dark room, Lea quickly saw the
reason.

Their bodies had begun decomposing, revealing
the skeletons beneath. Fleshless hands with stick-
like, bony fingers hung out from the ends of their

sleeves. Their faces were skeletal too, locked i
hideous, open-jawed grins. Tiny pockets of greer
decaying flesh still clung in the crevices of thei
skulls.

The man had one eye in place, the other a deep
empty socket. The woman had no face at all. Strand
of spidery black hair snaked down from the top of he
yellowing skullbone. A huge black worm crawled ou
of an eye socket and dropped down the front of he
blouse.

As Lea started to scream, both skeletal figures leap
to their feet, bones rattling as they stood. The
staggered toward the door, toward Lea, their bon
hands outstretched.

Lea screamed again.

And felt Catherine slip into her body.

Distracted by the gruesome figures advancing o
her, Lea had lost her concentration just long enougl
for Catherine to get in.

And now she felt the heaviness, felt the weight o
Catherine sinking through her. Helpless once again
Catherine in control now.

"You fool!" Catherine shouted angrily. "Yo
fool!"

The two skeletons rattled closer, stumbling ove
their ill-fitting clothes, their hands outstretched, botl
pointing long, accusing fingers.

"I warned you not to open the door!" Catherine
cried. "Those are my parents!"

"So there you are, evil child!" whispered the wom
an, the sound that of dry, rushing wind.

"Stay back, ghouls!" Catherine screamed in Lea's voice.

But the skeletons moved with surprising agility.

The man's hand snapped out, and his dry, bony fingers wrapped themselves like snakes around Lea's throat.

chapter

25

"*E*vil child!" the woman cried, her voice whistling through her open throat.

Lea gagged as the man's fingers tightened around her throat. She couldn't breathe through her nose because the foul odor of decaying flesh choked her. She tried to pull away from the hideous, grinning skulls with their dark, cavernous eye sockets, but both of them had hold of her now.

Their cadaverous arms wrapped around her, smothering her in darkness, choking her with the sour smell of the dead, laughing triumphantly, dry huffs of silent laughter blowing through their open jaws.

They're going to swallow me up, Lea thought.

They're going to make me like them.

And as she thought this, and as she surrendered to the hard, bony forms that were attempting to smother her, Lea felt Catherine float away.

I'm going to die now, Lea thought. But Catherine will not die with me.

Her parents are going to kill me now, and Catherine will survive.

Lea began to see flashes of red, swirls of red, growing brighter and brighter as the skeletons hugged her, choked off her breath, and wrapped themselves around her.

And then she saw Catherine beside her, her eyes glowing red as fire, her mouth twisted in anger, pointing an accusing finger at Lea's attackers.

"They murdered me once!" Catherine screamed. "Now they want to murder me again!"

"You evil liar!" the woman shrieked in brittle fury.

The skeletal figures relaxed their death grip on Lea. Lea uttered a low cry and sank to her knees, frantically sucking air.

"You evil liar!" the woman repeated, turning her yellowed, eyeless skull on Catherine. "You murdered us both and locked us forever in this room. But we have waited here all these years for you. We vowed not to rest until we stopped your evil!"

Her eyes glowing even brighter, Catherine tossed back her head and started to laugh. But her laughter was cut short as both her parents leapt at her, bones clattering.

They circled her with their putrid, baggy clothes, the odor rising in a vapor of decay, parts of them dropping off, bones falling to the floor, as they swept around her.

Catherine disappeared inside this foul, murderous

hug. As Lea gaped in frozen horror, the vengeful ghouls hugged their daughter, wrapping her tighter and tighter in a furious, swirling grip, suffocating her

"Help me! Please—help me!" Catherine cried out to Lea.

Catherine's pale hand reached out from the smothering embrace of her parents. But a skeletal hand grabbed Catherine's hand and, with a violent jerk twisted the hand off and tossed it to the floor.

Catherine and Lea screamed at the same time.

Lea covered her ears and shut her eyes.

But she couldn't shut out Catherine's final scream —the scream of an animal caught in a death trap.

When the scream faded away, Lea opened her eyes As she stared in openmouthed horror, all three ghostly figures melted together in a glowing, malodorous ball of flame, which slowly vanished in a choking cloud of yellow, sulfurous smoke.

Sobbing in terror, still struggling to catch her breath, Lea stared at the thick yellow vapor as it rose to the attic ceiling.

Everything went red.

And then black.

She could feel herself sinking to the floor, but she couldn't do anything about it.

chapter

26

When she opened her eyes, she saw only white.

Is this heaven? she wondered.

It took Lea a while to realize that she was staring up at a ceiling.

And then her mother's face hovered into view.

"Lea? Are you awake?"

Her mother had tears in the corners of her eyes, and her chin trembled as she stared down at Lea.

"Are you awake?" her mother repeated.

And then, from somewhere nearby, Lea heard the voice of her father. "Stand back a little. Give her room to breathe."

"I'm alive?" Lea asked, confused. She felt weak.

"Of course you're alive, dear," her mother said, wiping the tears with her finger.

Lea realized she was lying on her back. She looked

down and saw that she was in an unfamiliar bed, covered with a sheet and light blue blanket.

"Where am I?"

"Shadyside General," her father said, moving closer. "You've been very sick, Lea."

"I have?"

"You've had such a high temperature. It was a hundred and six for three days," Mrs. Carson said, her voice quavering.

"How long have I been here?" Lea asked, closing her eyes. The bright lights reflecting off the shiny, white ceiling were hurting her eyes.

"Nearly a week," her father said softly. And then quickly added, "But you're going to be okay."

"You mean it was all just a dream?" Lea asked, opening her eyes, turning her head toward her parents. Her head throbbed when she moved it.

"A dream?" Mrs. Carson was obviously confused.

"Did you have a lot of dreams?" Mr. Carson asked. "Sometimes when you have a high fever, you get very vivid and unusual dreams. They're called 'fever dreams.'"

"It was all a fever dream?" Lea asked.

She tried to sit up, but her entire body protested, and she groaned and sank back onto the pillow.

"You're going to be okay," Mr. Carson repeated. "You're just weak from being in bed so long."

"You'll be home in no time," Mrs. Carson told her. "And Deena says she's been organizing all your homework so you'll be able to catch up."

"Oh, great," Lea moaned. "Thanks a bunch, Deena."

Mr. Carson laughed. "Sounds like you're already back to normal."

"A boy has been calling for you. Every day," her mother said. "Don Jacobs. He sounded very worried about you."

Lea smiled. It was so hard to concentrate. "I can't believe it was all a dream," she said, drifting back to sleep.

Lea's first thought upon returning home three days later was to climb up to the attic and check the secret room. But her parents insisted that she stay in bed a few more days, and they kept a close and constant watch on her. She couldn't sneak up there.

Finally she couldn't wait any longer. Awakening early on a Saturday morning before either of her parents had stirred, she crept out of bed, pulled on a robe and her rubber thongs, and made her way silently up to the attic.

Pale morning light filtered in through the circular window. The floorboards creaked as always beneath her silent tread.

Sure enough, the hidden bedroom was locked and boarded up still.

All a dream, Lea thought.

She stood there in the silence for a while, trying to sort out her feelings. She couldn't decide if she was relieved or disappointed.

165

Still feeling shaky, she turned away from the hidden room and climbed back down to her bedroom. On the way back to bed, she passed the oval mirror above her dresser and took a peek at herself.

"I really need a haircut," she told herself. "My bangs are down over my eyes. I look like some kind of mangy sheepdog."

And then something beside the dresser lamp caught her eye.

A black ribbon.

Lea picked it up with a trembling hand. She knew immediately what it was.

It was Catherine's black velvet hair ribbon.

She held it tightly in one hand, running the fingers of the other hand over the smooth velvet.

Catherine and her evil had been real, after all.

And the room above Lea's bedroom had held Catherine's parents, waiting patiently for a hundred years to get their revenge on their daughter.

Staring at the ribbon, Lea felt a stab of renewed horror.

Marci. Poor Marci, she thought.

Marci had been the final victim of Catherine's evil. And Lea had been partly to blame.

Feelings of regret flooded over Lea. Regret and sadness.

She knew this was a feeling she would have to live with for a long, long time.

Lea toyed with the ribbon, tying it and untying it around her hand.

Should she tell anyone where the ribbon came from?

No, she decided.

The secret bedroom must remain a secret. Another secret of Fear Street, a street of secrets.

She put down the ribbon and made her way downstairs to fix some breakfast.

About the Author

R. L. STINE doesn't know *where* he gets the ideas for his scary books! But he wants to assure worried readers that none of the horrors of FEAR STREET ever happened to him in real life.

Bob lives in New York City with his wife and eleven-year-old son. He is the author of nearly twenty bestselling mysteries and thrillers for Young Adult readers. He also writes funny novels, joke books, and books for younger readers.

In addition to his publishing work, he is Head Writer of the children's TV show "Eureeka's Castle," seen on Nickelodeon.

WATCH OUT FOR

FEAR STREET®

SUPER CHILLER

SILENT NIGHT

Reva has always had it easy. She's rich, beautiful—and spoiled. But this time she's gone too far. Now someone has some surprises in store for her. Robbery? Terror? Even murder? Someone wants to treat Reva to a holiday she'll never forget! Holiday cheer turns to holiday chills for Reva. Someone is stalking her—someone wants revenge. Her money can't help her. No one can.

R.L. Stine